Detroit Tales

Detroit
Tales

Jim Ray Daniels

Michigan State University Press • *East Lansing*

☉ The paper used in this publication meets the minimum requirements
of ANSI/NISO Z39.48-1992 (R 1997) (Permanence of Paper).

Michigan State University Press
East Lansing, Michigan 48823-5245

Printed and bound in the United States of America.

08 07 06 05 04 03   1 2 3 4 5 6 7 8 9 10

LIBRARY OF CONGRESS CATALOGING-IN-PUBLICATION DATA
Daniels, Jim, 1956–
Detroit tales / Jim Ray Daniels.
p. cm.
ISBN 0-87013-662-3 (pbk.: alk. paper)
1. Detroit (Mich.)–Fiction. I. Title.
PS3554.A5635 D48 2003
811'.54–dc21

ACKNOWLEDGMENTS
Connecticut Review: "Renegade"
Gulf Stream: "Karaoke Moon"
Kestrel: "Cross Country"
The MacGuffin: "The Jimmy Stewart Story"
Natural Bridge: "Fireworks"
North American Review: "Minding the Store"
Our Working Lives: Short Fiction of Work, ed. Bonnie Jo Campbell, Larry Smith
(Huron, Ohio: Bottom Dog Press, 2000): "Bonus"
Tampa Review: "Islands"
West Branch: "Christmasmobile"
Witness: "Middle of the Mitten"

Cover design by Heather Truelove Aiston
Book design/layout by Sharp Designs, Inc.

Cover photograph is of the Memorial to Joe Louis by Robert Graham
located at Woodward Avenue and Jefferson in Detroit, MI.

■

Visit Michigan State University Press on the World Wide Web at **www.msupress.msu.edu**

Contents

Detroit Tales

Islands

We didn't live in the best neighborhood, but Sharon and I tried to make it better. I suppose you could've lumped us in with the "urban homesteaders," though I was never as idealistic as most of those folks. We bought there, in the heart of Detroit, because we got a lot of house for our money, and I figured I'd save more by walking to work. I never counted on the added advantage of being able to buy drugs right across the street.

Those urban homesteaders wouldn't get that joke, or they'd be afraid to laugh at it. Once they move in, they suddenly get worried about things like property values—they want to be able to bail out if they have to. We lived there eight years before we bailed out ourselves.

I work downtown, a short walk from Millview Avenue, our old street. I prided myself on sticking it out in the city while my coworkers were moving out to Rochester Hills or Bloomfield Hills or the Hilly-hill Hills. Anywhere up and away from what they see as the dregs at the bottom of the bowl. We used to call people who moved to the suburbs *quitters*. Now, we just shrug.

■ ■ ■

Directly across the street from our house, we had what the police refer to as a *problem building*—an old, run-down apartment complex. The wood façade was peeling off, its warped boards occasionally falling to the weeds below. A group of young men sat on the steps every night drinking. The faces changed, but the group remained. One guy used to pull his jeep up on the sidewalk and blare his car stereo directly toward our house. I kept waiting for his battery to run down. I could be waiting still.

The building was half-empty until the owner worked out a deal with Eastern Psych and they moved some patients in, turning part of it into a kind of halfway house. They'd shuffle up and down the street and rarely made a peep. My wife's friend Cheryl, a nurse, said they're mostly manic-depressives. Their slow walk they call the Thorazine shuffle. We had those people and the drug dealers in the same building. I could have lived with the crazies.

Sharon had Abe, our first child, almost two years ago, and she was pregnant again last summer, our last summer in that house. With Abe, we weren't getting any sleep, even without the noise from across the street. I understand it gets hot in those tiny efficiency units. I understand how they get driven out onto the steps. I understand a few beers on a hot night—I'm trying not to sound like some conservative hoo-ha. But then I started noticing needles and crack vials sprouting like deadly weeds on the traffic islands, *our* islands. Traffic was pulling up and leaving like the building was some kind of drive-thru all-night drugstore. With crack and heroin, it's always hot out. Those people are always thirsty and desperate. Every night, the market was open, and the guy with the Jeep, with those super-thumping bass speakers, he provided the Musak. My house shook with it.

I've been in journalism fifteen years now. I moved here from Lansing, the state capital, where I covered politics. That's where I got jaded. I used to be a true-blue Democrat. Now, I don't even vote. Sharon thinks I still vote, but on Election Day, I just go for a walk and pretend. I look at the sun, if the sun's out that day, and try and think about life as a simple thing. I cover high school sports now.

Six years ago, we—the folks on our block who cared—took over maintenance of the traffic islands in the middle of our street, lining them with Belgian blocks the city gave us from old streets they'd dug up and paved. We got the city to replace the dead trees, and we planted juniper bushes, flowers. The islands looked great, even if we had to fish the occasional needle or vial out of the dirt while weeding. Shortly before I gave in to Sharon and agreed to move, I found a switchblade. An antique—the guy probably realized those don't do much good anymore with everybody packing guns. I picked it up and dropped it in my garbage bag of weeds, but later I picked it out and wiped my fingerprints off.

Yeah, the building was making me a little nuts. At night, I sat at the dark window watching the drug deals while Sharon slept. Cars pulling up, engines idling. I often asked myself, Why don't the cops bust these guys? I always thought it'd be easy enough to bust a drug dealer, particularly when I was dealing drugs myself in between high school and college, but the truth is the cops don't really care until somebody gets shot or something. They're as cynical as the politicians: "They'll be out selling drugs in the same place tomorrow, or maybe move a couple blocks over." "There's no room in the jail." "These things take time." "Call the feds." "Call your neighborhood beat cop." "Call the drug enforcement division." "Call your councilman—maybe he can put some heat on my boss so I can give this some attention." We heard it all.

Last spring, I planted cosmos and coreopsis on the island directly in front of our house—bright, delicate, orange and yellow flowers. They do well in direct sun. I liked those names too—a touch of the exotic for our little island. There were five islands on the street. Since we lived across from the apartment building, we had to maintain one island all by ourselves, carefully tending it as we waited for the juniper bushes to fill in and choke out the weeds. Choke out the weeds. That's the metaphor I got stuck on, out there on my hands and knees watching the drug deals.

■ ■ ■

One Sunday morning when I was pushing Abe in the stroller, heading out to the park, I noticed a cleared square of dirt out on our island. It was mid-July—a little late to be planting anything. I picked up the empty seed packet nearby to show Sharon when I got home. I can't remember the name of those flowers now—they were purple in the picture on the packet. It was nothing like cosmos.

"Look what I found on the island," I said. I held up the seed packet, but she didn't look. She took Abe from the arm I had him cradled in.

"Not another needle?" she groaned. "Just don't tell me about it. I don't want to know about anymore of that shit till we get out of here." Sharon had been ready to pack it in since the murder-suicide in the building right before Abe was born. On Sundays, she'd started taking drives through new developments out in the suburbs, visiting open houses. I refused to go along. I refused to look at the sheets of computer printouts she shoved under my nose.

"Don't swear in front of Abe," I said. "He's going to start talking soon." Abe looked attentive in his high chair. He recognized his own name already.

"You're telling me not to swear, but you want your kids growing up across the street from drug dealers . . . I don't know where your head's at these days." Neither did I. I felt like I had a slow leak and could never get full enough to go anywhere.

"Just look," I said. I walked across the kitchen and handed her the packet. A couple of tiny seeds dropped to the floor.

Sharon fixed Abe a bottle. She was starting to show. I loved the smooth roundness of her belly, the perfect hill rising above all the garbage around us. I didn't blame her for going to the open houses, but I couldn't bring myself to consider the suburbs. There had to be some alternative in the city, and pretty soon maybe I'd start looking.

Sharon was distracted in the way only new and pregnant mothers can be. She was focused on her body and what was going on in there. She looked quickly at the envelope and pushed it back into my hands.

"Maybe it blew down the street. Maybe they were planting at the other end of the street."

"No, no, the dirt was turned over. It looks like somebody planted something on my island."

"Your island?"

"Well, yeah, when it comes to weeding it and all that. You don't see our friends across the street pitching in . . ."

"They're not our friends. Don't even joke about that."

Cocaine had been Sharon's drug of choice. I used to call her Hoover the way she vacuumed it up. She never liked pot—it made her paranoid. We'd slowed down a lot in recent years, but once she got pregnant, we stopped everything. She even made me give up pot. I still miss it. I'm always paranoid, so pot seemed to level me out, let the obsessions fall away. I'd never tried crack or heroin. No one I knew looked as hard or as desperate as the people pulling up across the street.

I looked out the window at the small square of earth. It looked like an animal had been digging. Sharon took Abe upstairs.

"I guess we'll see if anything grows there," I said to myself in that big empty room.

I tried to imagine anyone in the building caring about flowers— maybe the poor Chinese family, the grandparents caring for the large-headed baby. They smiled at us and said "hi" because that seemed to be the only word of English they knew. People pushing strollers, they say "hi" to each other more than anyone else in this world. It's like, "hey, we're in this together." It doesn't last long. Soon enough, the kids are punching each other out, the parents cheering them on.

The next day as I left for work, I saw one of the psych patients holding two blue plastic grocery bags stuffed with other grocery bags. She paced slowly back and forth in front of the clear patch of dirt, guarding it. It was always quiet on the street when I left for work. It seemed like a kind, benevolent world then, all danger still sleeping.

I don't know how she planted those seeds. Clawing with her hands, I guess.

"Did you plant these flowers?" I asked, pulling the packet out of my pocket.

"Yeah." Her thick face reddened, and she stared at the earth. A long, faded blue dress hung above her ankles. She was barefoot, and her feet were bruised with dirt.

I surprised myself then. "They sure are beautiful," I said.

She burst out laughing. "You're joking me. There ain't no flowers yet." She emphasized *yet* in such a strange way, as if a completely different person had said it.

■　■　■

She hung out with another shuffler, this guy with scraggly long hair and a scarred, haunted face. I called him Manson and her Janis. They looked like old hippies who'd had one too many acid trips, and who knows, maybe they were. Me, I was never one for acid. I didn't like the world in that many pieces.

They were usually arguing, her head lowered, his voice raised, as they shuffled down the street. He seemed sad and vulnerable until he started talking—then, the venom spewed out, random and vile. She didn't live with Manson, but they were clearly connected somehow. He lived alone on the first floor facing the street, and he stood at the window looking out with his Shroud of Turin stare.

They wore beat-up clothes, but it wasn't a fashion statement like when I was in college, and they both had the bad teeth of the real poor. She was missing her two front ones, so when she smiled, the big gap jumped out at me, some dark place I didn't want to visit. She looked like one of the innocents of this world, the kind the rest of us swallow up. The few times we spoke, she sounded childlike, though it was probably her medication talking.

Once before Abe was born, I'd been out walking the dog after work when I ran into her. She said, "What a pretty dog. What kind of dog is it?"

I started to answer, but she interrupted, saying again, "It's a pretty dog."

"Yes," I said, "that's what kind it is—a *pretty* dog."

She stood, shuffling in place. She hesitated before every move, every gesture, as if some crucial link in her brain was missing, as if the next move she made would crush her forever. She always looked like she'd been crying, her eyes red and puffy, her hair disheveled and knotted. The gap-toothed smile came as a complete surprise when it appeared. Like a flower blooming. A not particularly attractive flower, but a flower all the same.

After that, every time I saw her she asked, "Where's your pretty dog?" Long after we'd given him away after he bit Abe.

■ ■ ■

It was an extremely hot summer, and the weathermen were ecstatic, reeling off record highs from their air-conditioned studios. On Millview, we were wilting. Our cosmos and coreopsis were thriving, however, the envy of the neighbors down the way who'd planted less-hardy varieties. Janis watered her bare patch of dirt every day. I'd notice a dark spot from the water, as if a dog had peed there.

I had been planning on painting the trim out front for weeks, but kept using the heat as an excuse. Saturday was the day I promised Sharon I'd get to it, no matter how hot it was. When I awoke that morning, I was startled by the clarity of the blue sky. None of that summer haze. It had been a rough night with Abe, who'd been up at least a half-dozen times. It was my job to get up with him. Sharon had enough to worry about.

Rocking Abe at the window, I'd watched the drug deals—it'd been pretty lively, the regulars plus the weekenders stopping by. The little guy—whom I pegged as a gofer for the main dealer hidden in the building—was gliding back and forth to cars, sliding the money into a pocket, slipping vials into hands. From my second-floor perch, I felt like I was watching a movie I could not stop. I was stuck in that theater, and even if I walked away from the window, I knew the movie was still going on out there.

As I drifted off to sleep, I thought I heard Janis scream—I recognized her peculiar rasp. Or maybe it was a laugh. I listened for something else, but heard only Sharon's soft breathing. I lay in bed thinking about how the shell of the heart hardens over time. When I was younger, it shattered so easily when love rose up and flattened me. The sleep I lost, the tears I shed. It almost seemed quaint now. I thought about Janis, the Thorazine queen, and what shortened her stride.

That night, I admitted to myself that we should move. If Sharon was still working, we would easily have been able to afford it. As a teacher in the public schools with a master's degree, she'd made substantially more than I did. When we decided to have kids, we also decided Sharon would stay home until they were old enough for school, then go back to work.

Did I tell you how beautiful Abe is? Blue eyes and blond, almost white hair. Very fair skin—from Sharon's side. He smiled at me as I headed out in my painting clothes and goofy baseball hat from the school Sharon had taught at, the Watersmeet Nimrods. The hat had always made me silly and playful, but on that day, I pulled the brim down tight.

I climbed up on the long extension ladder that I'd set precariously on one of the steps up to the porch. I hated that job—the gutters and trim out front—it was already the second time I had to paint it since we moved in. I was so scared the first time, I'd done a lousy job. On the side of the house, I had to try to brace and level the ladders, since the driveway and front yard were angled at a steep slope, and in the front, I either had to put the ladder on a narrow porch step or in the middle of our dogwood tree. I'd put it off too long—paint was peeling in long strips, like layers of rock in the geology class I'd taken in college from old Dr. Hesske. He'd start in with his little hammer and forget the rest of us were there, forget he was teaching a class at all.

I wished for that kind of obliviousness. The drug runner was sitting on the stoop of the apartment building, soaking in the sun. I called him Secret Squirrel—he was short and skittish. Unlike the Thorazine shufflers, he was always alert. His head moved quickly back and forth, scoping out the street.

Around mid-morning, the neighbor I called the Boss walked by. Since we fixed up the islands, the Boss was always walking up and down the street, picking up every little bit of paper, every stray bottle, needle, cigarette pack. We had the Boss Patrol, the Secret Squirrel Patrol, and the Janis Patrol, everybody looking out for something else. I wondered if they had a name for me, and what it might be.

"You sort of let things go, didn't you?" the Boss said. Okay, his name is Ronald ("please don't call me Ron").

I thought that called for a "Fuck you, Ron." He didn't have any kids. He didn't know a thing about how that changes everything, how you don't have time to pick up every little scrap of paper, paint the second it needs to be done. I was conscious of the little guy across the street hearing every word we said.

Up on the ladder, I blew out a tense sigh. The day was heating up. I looked down at his blue business suit and smug silk tie. His bald spot was clearly visible from up there, though he worked hard to cover it.

"Yeah," I said. "Can't afford to hire somebody." That was close enough to a "Fuck you," I suppose. Ronald had paid someone to plant his flowers. I have no idea, absolutely no idea, why he bought a house on that street and sunk a ton of money into it. Ronald was a computer whiz who grew up in Detroit, made a lot of money in the Silicon Valley, then quit and moved back. He didn't even work for a couple of years. He supervised the renovations on his house— drove the workmen crazy, I'm sure. Then he either got bored or had miscalculated his income, because he had taken a job as some kind of troubleshooter for an electrical engineering firm downtown.

"Any vials today?" I said to him loudly. He quickly turned and looked at the dealer across the street. He was in denial about the drugs. It wasn't the kind of problem he could solve with his skills for designing software and picking up garbage. He shook his head and hurried off toward his own house. After the sleepless night with Abe, I was slopping paint all over the place, splashing it on and hoping for the best, hoping we'd be gone before it had to be painted again.

The street was quiet all morning as I worked, so I was surprised when I turned around near noon to see the little guy still sitting on the stoop. I often saw him hanging out by the bank of phones around the corner by the Unimart. I never understood why they needed four pay phones there. It's like the drug dealer put in an order for them. The main dealer seemed to be this tall, thin guy who always wore sunglasses and a hat. He slipped in and out so quietly, you had to be watching carefully to even know he lived there. His apartment on the second floor in the front gave him the perfect vantage point to watch the street. I sometimes glimpsed his shadow near the curtains, my evil twin, watching the street with me.

Wasps had been bothering me all morning, and I was slowly moving across the front of the house closer to their nest. Suddenly, one shot out from the eaves and buzzed my head. I slapped at it with the paintbrush. The brush flew from my hand and landed on the driveway, leaving a trail of white paint on the cement. I heard a laugh behind me. I clenched my teeth. I knew I'd have to get down and clean up what I could. It was close to lunchtime. I needed a break.

■　■　■

"It's not worth it," one cop told me—an undercover narc who actually came out to meet me.

"Great location," he said, looking out my front windows.

"Thanks," I said.

"No, for a drug dealer," he said. "Access to the park for quick escapes, right off a main road for convenience. I bet they love it here. The building gives them cover too—makes it harder to pinpoint where things are happening."

He said he might look into it once he finished working on the West Side, but we never saw him again.

At the last Block Watch meeting, one of the older residents had suggested, "Why don't you just talk to them, ask them to move on?" A couple people laughed out loud. "You can't just talk to them," I said. I'd read about a guy in Cleveland who tried that—the next time he left his house, somebody burned it down. But on a peaceful summer morning, everything quiet, I felt stupid enough to believe that maybe one human being could talk to another.

Weak and dizzy, I slowly descended the ladder, my heart pounding wildly. Too hot to paint. I retrieved the brush and scrubbed at the spilled paint with a rag. I heard a buzzing behind me and turned to see the wasp struggling, white paint weighing down its wings. I smiled, then squashed it. I wrapped the brush in aluminum foil, then, instead of heading into the house, I walked across the street, my head down, my Nimrods hat shading my eyes. My belly stung from scraping it on shingles to paint the corners of the porch. I briefly looked back at the house. The green bushes under the gutters were already splattered with white. It looked like snow. The day was turning upside down.

I walked over to the stoop and sat down, as I had imagined doing many times before. "Hot," I said. My hands were covered with white paint. I quickly tried to peel some of the bigger, dried pieces off.

"You're the guy always watching over here," he said, and everything I had thought to say got sucked out of my lungs in a flash. I sat there silently.

"Got that wasp, eh?" He chuckled again.

"I'm Gerry," I said. I didn't say "with a 'G' " like I did with most people. He'd never be writing my name down for anything. I reached out my paint-covered hand, but he didn't take it.

"Name's Steve," he said. "Man, you best be washing those hands."

I just wanted to quietly get up and walk back across the street, back to my side of the island. I'd imagined coming to terms with this guy. I thought I could make him understand that I'm a normal, reasonable human being—a guy who had used a few drugs in his day, not some crazed vigilante narc.

"We think," I said quickly, "we think somebody's selling drugs in this building."

"Maybe you're right," he said, leaning back again on his elbows. He was even shorter once you got next to him—5'4" maybe.

"I'm just trying . . . I got a kid, you know," I said.

"I know," he said, "and that damn dog."

We'd given the dog away a month ago. I let that pass. "Don't want my kid growing up with drugs across the street."

"Drugs across every street in America, my man," he said.

"I don't want him caught in the crossfire when the shooting starts. You don't know who's got a gun these days." I tried not to look him over. His clothes were loose. A small gun could fit anywhere.

He cracked a thin smile. "Everybody got a gun these days, that's who."

"I don't want no trouble," I said. "I'm just a guy painting his house."

"Who taught you how to paint, man?" he laughed. "Look at you."

What did he know about painting? I wanted to wring his skinny little neck, though I hadn't been in a fight since ninth grade. I was thirty-five, and my hair was prematurely gray. Sharon wanted me to dye it, but I was ready to look older than I was, to look as old as I felt. I glanced up at the second-story window, but with the sun's glare, I couldn't see if the dealer was there, though I caught a glimpse of Manson standing in his window directly behind me, spreading his arms like Jesus on the cross.

The Chinese family exited the building, passing us quickly and silently, carrying the kid with the giant head. By the time he'd be old enough to play with Abe, they'd be living somewhere else, I thought. Or we would.

"See, they mind their own business," Secret Squirrel said.

"They probably think you're selling candy out here," I said.

"They don't think," he said. "That's your problem. Man don't want trouble should mind his own business. Ain't nobody getting hurt over here. Nobody on this street getting hurt," he said. He yawned to make his point. I was suddenly very tired. He wouldn't shoot me in broad daylight in front of my own house, I told myself. I'd never seen my house from this perspective, never studied it closely. It was a big old house, a little clunky and boxy, the bricks dirty with years of factory soot.

"You go home and take care of your wife and kid," he said. "We'll take care of things over here." He looked me in the eye.

I stood up. I don't know what made me say it. Maybe I was just trying to wake myself up.

"I've got a gun," I said.

He might have even believed me, but I doubt it. This wasn't about being tough. It was about doing business. Secret Squirrel and his friends didn't want to shoot anybody because it'd mess up business. It'd be a complication. "It's not worth it," he said. "Gerry, it's not worth it."

"Yeah," I said. I felt my shoulders slumping, pulling me down. I headed back across the street. I knew I couldn't do any more painting that day. I felt like one of those losing coaches I interviewed so often—"I feel bad for the kids, they worked their butts off to get here." I didn't know anybody's real name in that building—maybe I was already living in the suburbs and didn't know it.

In the basement, I cleaned my brushes at the washtubs. Sharon was putting Abe down for a nap and then taking one herself. The heat really zapped her. I'd left the job half-finished, but I just couldn't climb back up the ladder again that day. When I went upstairs, they were both sleeping peacefully. I sat on the edge of the bed and wept.

■ ■ ■

"What are you doing, standing in the street talking to a nut like that?" Sharon said one day in late July after I'd been out weeding the island. Janis was hard to avoid. Every time I weeded, she'd come down to watch me, to ask about the pretty dog that no longer existed. "Abe needs a bath." She handed him to me and left the room. She was right to put our small child in my hands then. Abe's like a touchstone to what's best in me.

Sharon used to have more urban homesteader in her, but when you don't have kids, you can afford more idealism. Ronald isn't going to have kids, I can tell, even if he can find someone to marry. Sharon had a new edge to her that cut through the fat layers of bullshit that clogged those streets. "A lot of the world shuts down when you're pregnant," she said to me, and I could see it happening. I hadn't told her about my talk with Secret Squirrel.

Later that week, Sharon and I went for a walk one evening after it cooled down a bit. I'd started looking for Secret Squirrel before I went outside. I was trapping myself in my own house. We put Abe in the stroller and headed for the park. Janis intercepted us in the street, on her side of the island. She was carrying a water glass to spill on her plot of earth. Nothing had emerged from the dust yet. She was trying to make something beautiful there, just like us.

Janis didn't stop so much as put her shuffle into neutral, moving but not going anywhere, alone in front of us with her ever-present plastic grocery bag.

"Is that your family," she asked.

I nodded, "Yes, yes, we're a family."

She said, "Me too," and put her hand on her belly. "Three months," she said.

We both looked at Janis's loose blouse—missing a button in the middle, a glimpse of pale flesh. I couldn't imagine what'd be in store for any child she might have. I doubted Human Services would let her keep a baby. I stared at her belly, not wanting to believe, but it looked like something might be growing there. It was like looking at Secret Squirrel's shirt to see if there was a gun tucked beneath it. "Congratulations," Sharon said, and Janis blushed.

She spilled her glass of water on the hard dirt, and it splattered up on my shoes. I looked down again at her square of dirt and noticed the tiny green sprout of a familiar weed. I pushed the stroller away toward the park. "Hey, where's that pretty dog?" she shouted after us.

"On the moon," Sharon shouted back.

"She's not pregnant," Sharon said to me as we turned into the park. "No way."

"Do you think she could make up that blush," I asked.

"Maybe it's sunburn," Sharon said. "Look, I'll bet you she isn't. If you're wrong, we have to move."

"What if you're wrong?" I asked. "Do we stay?"

"If I'm wrong, then you can name the next baby," she said, stroking her belly.

Within a month, however, Janis disappeared, as those from Eastern Psych did, without a trace. I still saw her friend Manson, swaying on the steps of the building, as shell-shocked and morose as ever. I wanted to ask him about Janis, but I didn't want to know, not really. Our orange flowers bloomed all down the island, spreading like weeds, like the heartiest flowers do. A mess of beautiful orange heads waving gaily, mocking us with false hopes for a bright future as a family there. A little island paradise surrounded by cement, by waves of passing cars, garbage floating up on its shores, picked at by scavengers, collectors, and dogs desperately marking their territory. In late August, in that small cleared patch, a group of hearty weeds had taken over.

Like Janis, we've moved on, so I'm writing this from someplace safe. Abe plays in our fenced-in yard. We lost the second child at the end of the summer. I paid someone to finish painting. We moved before Christmas. We're trying to have another child. I look out my window onto the perfect green square of my lawn and the ordered silence of our street. I wonder who's taking care of the island now.

One night shortly after Janis disappeared, we were heading out for another walk in the park. The "For Sale" sign was up in front of our house. Secret Squirrel was sitting on the steps. He nodded at me. "Hey, Gerry," he said softly. What was I trying to wipe off that switchblade? God, I'm not sure. I wish life was as simple as seeing a purple flower bloom.

Sharon just looked at me, as if I'd been keeping something from her, and I had been. I didn't look back. I looked at him.

"Steve," I said. It's all I had to say, then I nodded.

Minding the Store

Carl Jacks was the kind of guy who got drunk and beat up his own friends, so you can imagine he didn't have a lot of them. We were all afraid of him, and I think he figured that was just as good.

At a party in Mound Park, Carl had punched out two of his buddies who were trying to convince him not to drive home. Mound Park was off Eight Mile Road, the border between Detroit and Warren, and it took police from both cities to take care of Carl. He took a few clunks on the head. But Carl had an incredibly hard head and incredible luck—the police decided to let him go. His friends wouldn't press charges.

I worked at the Jolly Giant Party Store, which was close enough to our high school to get a lot of kids trying to pass themselves off as eighteen, the drinking age in Michigan back then. I was only sixteen myself, but the owner—this crazy guy named Charles who had Little Richard's thin mustache and some of his flamboyance—liked me and gave me a job. I used to stop in every day after my paper route for an Orange Crush and some chips and listen to him bullshit about how to fix the world. Charles lived with his friend, Marcel, who was always formal and serious. He was a CPA and did the books for a lot of the local businesses. I never saw him without a suit on.

None of the customers knew about Marcel. Charles, for all his flamboyance, kept the whole sexual thing in check. He knew what kind of neighborhood his store was in—a working-class area on the edge of Detroit—and he wanted to stay in business. The video store next door had a waiting list for those Real Death videos—spliced-together clips of people getting killed. I never had the stomach for that shit. Maybe that's why Charles liked me.

I thought it was pretty weird, Charles and Marcel, and what they might do together at home, but I never saw them touch each other, and they never bothered me, and I never told a soul about what I knew.

Marcel came in every night at closing time to help shut things down. He called me Mr. Cummings. He had the faintest wisp of a smile, and I usually saw it after Charles said something clever. You could tell they loved each other just by the silence between them. Charles's other employee, Martha, an old Polish woman, was a carryover from the previous owner. "Those two," she'd say to me, and roll her eyes at Charles and Marcel. Her husband had lost an arm in an industrial accident and was home on disability. Her only son was an alcoholic in and out of trouble with the cops. A couple of guys shacking up? "Eh," she'd say, "they seem happy."

So, there I was, checking i.d.'s when I wasn't old enough to drink myself. I was never tempted to sell to my underage friends: Charles had given me responsibility. He trusted me, and I didn't have much else going for me back then—I had bad acne, and I was scrawny as hell. I'd wanted to play football but could never gain enough weight, despite plenty of peanut butter-and-banana milkshakes.

I knew that I was never going to kick anybody's ass, so when Carl Jacks came in the store, I was probably more afraid than the time Charles and I got robbed. Carl pushed his way in at around seven on a Friday night. It was still light outside, but judging from Carl's behavior at some of the parties I'd been to, he usually started pretty early.

He came straight for me, though I was at the candy counter selling Flying Saucers and Lucky Suckers to the Deveraux girls who lived around the corner.

"Hey man, I need some Mad Dog."

Mad Dog, Mister Death, whatever you wanted to call it. I never heard anyone ask for it by its official name, Mogen David 20/20. Twenty percent alcohol. Wino wine for the new generation.

I swallowed hard, as if I was actually trying to eat one of those hard, dry Flying Saucers. At that moment, I wanted to be flying away in one.

"Uh, yes, yes, we do—on the shelf there." I almost called him *sir.* I pointed behind me. It was against the law to chill the fortified wines—wines 20 percent alcohol or higher counted as hard liquor. Charles didn't sell any cold wine, period. He didn't want it to become a wino store. That was the kind of compromise he'd make—sell it, but not cold, so he wouldn't sell very much of it.

Carl swiveled, then turned back quickly. Every small gesture seemed full of menace. "I mean *cold.*"

"We don't carry it cold. It's against the law."

He shook his head as if trying to comprehend that astounding bit of information. When Carl got crazy at a party, he'd shake his head like that, wandering in circles, deliberately crashing into people.

But there wasn't much room to wander in the Jolly Giant, and he was sober, so he grabbed two warm bottles and set them on the checkout counter. I stood frozen with the cute little Deveraux girls looking up at me. The younger one, Darlene, had snot streaming into her mouth as she waited expectantly for me to hand over the box of Lucky Suckers.

Charles stood behind the deli counter slicing some Polish ham. "Bob Ray, will you get that?" I should explain about the name Bob Ray—it was a phase I was going through . . . well, maybe later.

"Shit," I said under my breath. "Listen girls, I've got to wait on that man over there. I'll be right back." The Deveraux girls would do anything for me. They nodded solemnly. Working the candy counter, now *that* was real power—everything desired under glass, and I stood behind it.

I was trying to get to the checkout counter fast enough to keep Carl from getting too pissed off but slow enough to figure out a strategy. He was only a junior, so I didn't think he was eighteen.

I looked over at Charles. He was watching me, the meat slicer idly whickering the air. I looked over at the Deveraux girls. Little Darlene was licking off the snot and swallowing.

"Do you have any i.d.?" I nearly whispered.

Carl thought that was a good joke. He stood there laughing to himself. Carl could have made a good linebacker, but he was more on the bar bouncer career track, and that was only if he could get himself under control.

"Wait a minute," he said, and turned and went outside back to his car.

As soon as he was out of the store, I turned to Charles. "Hey Charles, this guy's gonna come back in and kill me. You want to take over?" He concentrated on the meat slicer as if he didn't hear me.

Before I knew it, Carl stomped back into the store and tossed his driver's license across the counter at me.

Not only was he eighteen, he was nineteen. I should have known somebody like Carl had been held back a time or two. One more time, and he'd be in my class. Right then, I made a silent prayer he wouldn't fail again.

"Thank you," I said, and gently pushed the license back toward him.

After I'd bagged the bottles and given him his change, he leaned toward me. I was wrong—he'd already started drinking. "Next time, keep some cold ones for me, okay, buddy?"

"Sure," I said, just happy to keep my pimply face intact for another day.

He exploded out the door. I looked out the window and saw a couple freshman girls sitting in the back seat of his rust-bucket Chevy.

"Oh Lord, save them," I said aloud, then I felt little sticky fingers on mine, and I turned and waited on the Deveraux girls.

■ ■ ■

Flying Saucers were pale, multicolored wafers with little balls of hard candy rolling around in the middle. The wafers tasted like communion hosts. The balls tasted like small pebbles. Though they were awful, the kids loved them. They'd bite a hole in the side and pour the aliens down their throats. For a penny, you could be a monster. Not such a bad deal, I suppose.

Stocking the candy counter was one of Charles's favorite things about owning the store. The liquor paid the bills, but the candy filled Charles's bulging, sick heart. At the time, we didn't know it was sick. Charles ended up being the third person in the state of Michigan to get a heart transplant, and he lived five years with it, which was pretty good back then. Mysterious Marcel was with him to the end, soberly holding his hand then and not caring who saw.

Charles used to stand in front of the candy counter on the spot where the tile floors had been worn through down to bare cement.

"You know how many kids have stood here and pressed their faces against this glass and looked at this candy and put their golden pennies on the countertop and pointed their stubby little fingers and took their tiny paper bags and were happy?"

Charles liked to talk in long sentences. He imagined himself a poet, though he read the worst crap imaginable. Even I could tell that. One book was called *Thoughts about Myself, and Other Deep Mysterious Things.* No kidding. He loved the hell out of that one. He used to sit on beer cases in the back and read it aloud to me and Martha on slow rainy days in this phony voice I imagined he thought was super sensitive. We used to howl with laughter, and I think Charles laid it on thick just for us. He was the kind of guy who wanted to please, even if it meant making fun of himself. Listening to him read, laughing with Martha in that warm little store, I felt like I had a family. When I walked in the store every day after school, dropped my books, and put on my clerk's apron, it felt like home. I've never had another job in my whole life where I felt like that.

I knew Martha from when Mr. Gene owned the store. I used to think she was Mrs. Gene. The way Martha talked about him, I wondered if there hadn't been something going on between them. He'd died five years ago of leukemia, then the real Mrs. Gene sold the store to Charles. Martha treated me like a grandson. I think she'd always wanted another shot at mothering, so she was working on me. She was one of those people who could look the same for twenty years, so I really had no idea how old she was—maybe around sixty. Her cheeks were full of sass and good humor, and I loved her back just a little bit.

Charles let me do my homework when business was slow, and Martha always made sure I got it done. We often got takeout from Paul's Pizza around the corner. Charles always paid, and Martha and I, we let him. Sometimes she'd fry up some pierogi and kielbasa on the hot plate in the back room, and we'd have a little Polish feast. "I need to fatten you up, Bobby," she'd always say, as if a little weight was all I needed.

Though Charles complained about the smell of frying onions, he and I always fought over the odd last pierogi. Truth was, he loved them. When I think of that store, I think of the three of us eating off our laps. No customers. Well, maybe the Deveraux girls or Squeaky Kowalski or some of the neighborhood kids just hanging out, hoping somebody'd spill some change or toss them a pity nickel. But we'd just be sitting there, smiling and nodding at each other, chewing open-mouthed, our cheeks bulging with it. Martha used to say it was the best food in the world, and we never argued with her.

I did have a family, of course. I don't want to say much about them—it would sound like typical teenage whining: my parents don't understand me, blah, blah, blah. Okay—just a couple of things: my older brother and sister were one year apart, and my younger brother and sister were one year apart. I was in the middle, with four years between me and anyone else. My mother got me two department-store birds for my birthday one year, and they both died within a week. After the first one died, she got the other one a mirror for companionship. I think the second bird died from looking at himself so much, and I think that's what was killing me those years—too much looking in the mirror and not liking what I saw.

I don't know what my parents were doing during all those blank years on either side of me, but it seemed like my mother felt guilty about them, and my father angry. On my worst lonely nights, I felt like the black hole of the family. "Boo hoo, that's enough whining," as Charles would say. He never talked about his own family, and I didn't ask.

When you're sixteen, your own family is usually not what you want, no matter what they're like, so you wander into the world desperately looking for some other kind of community to accept and love you. Sometimes you end up like Carl, with fear and hatred instead. I could never find my spot on the social map of our school. I was one of the dumbest kids in the classes for smart kids.

I did have a girlfriend though. Jeanette. She was kind of homely, like me, but she had beautiful breasts that I could cup in my hands some nights after her trusting parents went to bed and left us alone in the living room watching TV. She liked my thinness, rubbing her hands up my shirt and over my ribs. When she'd come in the store, Charles always waited on her, elaborately bagging her purchases and putting the change in her hand, holding it till she turned red.

He knew I was insanely jealous. But it was just Charles, so I could laugh it off. He'd rig up the Land o' Lakes butter boxes so if you lifted the box the maiden was holding, it looked like you saw her breasts—they were her knees cut out from another box and taped on, if you're wondering. Charles had this weird breast fixation. Maybe he went both ways. I was just a kid and didn't know anything about gray areas.

"I love the sensuous," he said once. He had opened up a canned Polish ham and was scraping off the jelly it was packed in. I hated that job—all that cold, slimy crap gave me the creeps. "Oh, feel that meat. Oh, smell all that meat. It's so primal!"

"What's he going on about now?" Martha asked.

I burst out laughing. "Meat," I said.

"Oh, Lord," she said.

"Oh, yes!" Charles shouted in response. I didn't understand Charles, but I knew he had a good heart—well, maybe I mean "soul," the heart that counts, finally, in the end.

■ ■ ■

I started keeping a couple of cold Mad Dogs in the cooler for Carl, and he came in every Friday and Saturday night for them. When he entered the store, I hurried to the cooler and pulled out his Mad Dogs from where I'd hid them. Charles kept quiet about it. I think he'd heard the fear in my voice that first day. I doubt Charles'd had much success dealing with bullies himself.

Carl started calling me Bob Ray when he came in, so Charles

stopped calling me Bob Ray. Martha never called me Bob Ray. When I waited on Carl, she glowered at the both of us from her perch by the cigarette racks.

I'd complained to Charles one day about having a boring name: Robert Smith. He knew my middle name was Raymond from my pay stub and created Bob Ray to give me something a little more colorful. I liked it, though it never went beyond the store—like what I knew about Charles and Marcel. Now it had slipped out into the dangerous world of Carl Jacks.

Carl had been in my gym class the previous year, and I was a witness to one of the most famous Carl Jacks stories. We all had to box. You got paired off by weight, then went at it. I boxed Rich Dunn, and we each got a C+, two scrawny kids flailing at each other with those heavy gloves. Coach Burns laughed and smiled when we were done. "Well, wasn't that cute?" he said.

One day Coach Burns was showing us some boxing moves while we sat sprawled on the mats, bored and indifferent. We knew none of that stuff would do us much good out on the street. Carl was yakking it up with some of the other goons when Coach stopped and slowly turned toward them, gave them his hard stare.

"Jacks, you think you know it all, you get up here and I'll demonstrate on you."

Carl slowly stood, laughing that stupid laugh to himself. He's the kind of guy who could kill somebody while smiling the whole time. Who knows, maybe he's done that by now—I lost track of him a long time ago. So, he put on the gloves and Coach said, "Okay, Jacks, now you try to hit me."

Carl laughed even harder. "Naw, this is a trick. I know it."

"No, come on, hit me." Coach said. "Try and hit me."

Carl's thick arms dangled at his sides, and he started to turn away from Coach, who relaxed just enough so that Carl could whirl around and deck him with a punch square on the nose.

All hell broke loose. Coach went after Carl, and they were duking it out when the athletic director and the other gym teachers came rushing out of the office to break it up. The rest of us just sat there. None of us were touching that. Coach had a busted nose. Carl looked okay as they hauled him away. "He told me to hit him," he kept saying, and laughing—he knew he had them. He was sent home for the rest of the day, then got permanently excused from gym class.

■ ■ ■

I'd never believed in pure evil. There had to be some good in everybody, right? I was beginning to think Carl had some good in him. I mean, he had punched out the worst tyrant of a teacher in the school and had gotten away with it—that gave him some hero points. There must've been something besides fear that made me try to please Carl. Something I didn't like but couldn't stop. I went out of my way to keep him happy. I felt good when he called me "Bob Ray." Maybe it was that I felt protected somehow, though I should have known better.

The Deveraux girls had been having bad luck with the Lucky Suckers, so one day I rigged it and put two winners right on top. They were digging their hands down deep to get the ones at the bottom, shuffling them around while I was trying to keep track of where the winners were. Little Darlene was over her cold, which seemed to last six months out of every year, and her sister, Kristy, was being nice to her for a change. Finally, I lost my patience. "Look, Darlene, you take this one, and Kristy, you take this one!"

They reluctantly took the suckers from my hand and glumly opened them. They both said "It's A Winner!" on the inside.

"Hey look, you both got winners!" I shouted, but they simply held them up and looked at me.

"You cheated," Kristy said. "It's no fun when you cheat."

"Yes," Charles echoed from across the store, "it's no fun when you cheat." Something was eating at him. He'd been quiet, even when we were alone in the store—hiding in the back room, keeping me busy with arbitrary cleaning chores.

I felt like pounding my fists on the glass countertop. "Does that mean you don't *want* your free ones?"

They looked at each other for a long second. "No, we'll take our free ones," Kristy said, and they both picked out another sucker, and they were both losers. Lucky Suckers tasted like weak, brittle Kool-Aid, but the chance of getting a free one kept them popular. The Deveraux girls were addicted to the two worst candies—Flying Saucers and Lucky Suckers. Their father was a drunk. Excuse me for making it sound like everybody was a drunk, but working in a liquor store, you knew. You knew whose hands shook; you knew whose eyes wandered over the rows of orderly bottles with sick lust.

Even Martha's son sometimes stumbled in to the Jolly Giant to mock his mother. To make her pull a bottle down and put it in a bag and take his money. It must have given him a perverse pleasure, one of the few of his dismal days. It made his mother sick. "I told you to take your business someplace else," she'd tell him in a monotone voice that wasn't her own. I think he usually did go somewhere else, but from time to time, he'd show up near closing to get one more bottle and taunt his mother. I'd watch helplessly while her cheeks sagged, her eyes filled with tears, and her whole body seemed to take on another twenty years. Charles was always gentle with her on those nights, draping her faded green sweater over her shoulders as he led her out the door, giving them a squeeze before she walked off alone toward home.

■　■　■

"What made you buy this place?" I asked Charles one day after Martha had gone home. It was a wonderfully cluttered store—a wide deli counter ran across the back wall, hard liquor lined the far wall, with the checkout in front of it alongside a bakery counter (fresh baked goods delivered daily from Oaza Bakery in Hamtramck) and, of course, the candy counter, which was wedged into a corner near the door. The candy and baked goods were in tall, slanted glass cases that Martha constantly cleaned in a losing battle against sticky fingerprints.

In the middle, we had two rows of canned groceries, and on the wall by the door, the beer and pop coolers, the dairy cooler, and the ice cream freezer. Below the front windows sat chips and Twinkies and other junk food. We sold just about everything. And when the fresh bread arrived in the morning, it smelled like heaven. Because of school, I missed most mornings, so every Saturday, Charles would let me tear into a fresh warm loaf. He called it Communion Time—he loved to watch me devour it. I shook my head like a dog with a shoe, the whole loaf in my mouth. I couldn't get enough of what that store gave me.

"I always liked the idea of the corner store, the neighborhood store, where you really get to know your customers," he said. He used to work selling men's clothes at an exclusive store out at Somerset, the fancy mall twenty miles to the west, twenty miles farther from the city. He inherited "a tidy sum," as he put it, when his mother died, and bought Gene's Jolly Giant. He hadn't changed the name, and newer customers called him Gene—or Mr. Jolly Giant, which Charles always loved, puffing up dramatically. Charles even loved the old red neon Jolly Giant sign out front, which flashed what was supposed to be a giant, though actually it looked more like a fat midget. He hadn't changed anything.

Charles's grandparents had owned a small corner grocery, and above his deli counter he hung an enlarged, blurry photo of them standing in that store. He had spent a lot of his childhood there. Charles knew it was never going to be that simple anymore. He railed against the large supermarkets. "Cow barns," he called them. "And we're the cows going to slaughter down the anonymous aisles while this country loses its soul. Loses its soul, I tell you."

"Amen," Martha'd say, rolling her eyes. Her eyes got a workout around Charles, but she needed a workout—every minute in that store was a minute away from her depressed husband and alcoholic son.

"He lost an arm, and they took his heart with it," she was fond of saying about her husband, Mike, and when he came by to walk her home some nights, and I saw his long, gloomy, defeated face, I could not argue with her. "He watches soap operas, for God's sake," she said once, nearly in tears. "The old Mike, he wouldn't have stood for that . . . Wouldn't have stood for a lot of things," and Charles and I, we both knew what she meant by that.

Charles had to sell booze to hang on to his nostalgic dream. He had to pay the devil. "I never really thought about dealing with the alkies," he said. "I knew the liquor license was what made the business go, but I never thought about what it would do to me to see those same desperate people every single day.

"Look," Charles said, "you don't see the tile worn all the way through in front of the liquor counter. You know why? The men and women who stand there have a name on their lips when they arrive and it's the name on one of those bottles behind you. Do you see hesitation? No. Do you see indecision? No. You see desperation and fear. And who gives them what they need? I do, Bob Ray. I am the Candy Man, you see? The kids, they don't know what they want. There's a whole beautiful world of sweetness there before them . . ."

I liked it when Charles talked to me like that, like an adult. He made himself vulnerable in ways that no adult I knew did. Everyone—parents, teachers—they all put on the front. They never admitted they were wrong.

■ ■ ■

After the Deveraux girls gave their suckers a few discouraged licks and wandered home, I said to Charles, "Are you mad at me about something?" I grabbed a penny pretzel and stuck it in my mouth to help keep a casual front.

"No, no," he said, then quickly, "yes. I mean, I am concerned about your relationship with Mad Dog Man."

"Relationship?" I laughed. "What, are you jealous?" I instantly regretted saying those words, but they were out there, hanging in the air of the small, cluttered store where there was no getting them back.

After a long silence, Charles's voice turned hard and cold. "I don't want you keeping any more cold Mad Dog for that boy." He said "boy" with a dismissive sneer.

"He'll kill me," I whined. I was still trying to think of a way to take my smart-ass remark back, but I was sixteen and didn't know how.

Jeanette and I had broken up two weeks earlier, and I missed her with a sexual urgency and longing that I have trouble describing. She was my guide to a softer world. I'd seen her kissing another boy at a party and had grabbed her arm—a little rough, I think now. "Why?" I'd asked her.

"I'm drunk," she said. I had gone to the party sober after the store closed at ten. She'd been out with her friends for hours.

I didn't drink much. I think I was doing some strange kind of regressing, working in a liquor store but hanging out at a candy counter. I could eat all I wanted, and that turned out to be a lot. It was showing on my face. And I was seeing things in the store that most kids my age wouldn't see for a long time—the pale, bloated faces of alcoholics sometimes haunted my dreams.

"How'd you like it if I was out here kissing somebody else?" I looked around at the milling, swaying circles of teenagers. It looked like everybody was drunk.

"Oh, go ahead," she said, "kiss somebody else. Go ahead and kiss somebody," then she exploded with a shrill laugh that scared the shit out of me. I turned and walked away, and we hadn't spoken since.

"Robert," he said, "we have to stick up for ourselves in this world against the Mad Dog monsters who will rub our faces in the dirt and then make us pay them for the privilege. I cannot stand here and watch this go on any longer."

"He'll kill me," I repeated hopelessly. He put his hand on my shoulder, and I flinched, though I didn't mean to.

"I'll wait on him," Charles said, "like I should have the first time."

■　■　■

Carl came in Friday night, right on schedule. Most of the evening, I'd been hiding in the big walk-in cooler in the back, but Carl sniffed me out. Instead of asking Charles, who stood waiting for him at the counter, he'd started snooping around the cooler himself. He saw the walk-in door ajar and swung it open. I was sitting on a half-dozen cases of Pabst Blue Ribbon twelve-ounce cans.

"Oh, hi," I said. "Just cooling off."

"Knock it off, smart-ass. Where's my cold Dogs?"

I flinched as if he'd already hit me. He had me trapped. "We— the boss said we can't keep any . . . any more cold ones for you."

"Ah, shit, you pimple-faced pussy." He slammed the cooler shut, and I was locked in. I felt like I wouldn't mind freezing to death, but it wasn't to be that simple. He yanked the door open again and pulled me out by the collar.

"Can I help you with something?" It was not Charles but Martha who came out from behind the deli counter. What was Charles doing? He was visibly swaying, trying to steady himself against the checkout counter. Carl was still holding me. "Bob Ray, my man, what's the story here?"

"You let go of him," Charles pleaded, his voice cracking. "I'll call the police."

"And do what, tell them you got an underage punk like this selling booze?"

That stopped us all. We were used to the routine—if someone we didn't know came in, Martha or Charles would sell the liquor. Carl wasn't as stupid as he appeared. Mean and stupid weren't synonyms, though I had always wanted or imagined them to be. He must have willfully failed. I could see him doing that—failing—to spite the world.

I turned back to the walk-in and pulled out the one bottle I'd hidden as insurance, in defiance of Charles, and handed it to Carl.

"Just one?"

It was the kind of compromise I imagined Charles making. "Yeah—it's all we got left," I said, shrugging my shoulders up around my neck.

He silently took it up to the counter, then he grabbed a warm one off the rack and set it beside the cold one.

My heart was flipping like a stuck record. I couldn't imagine what Charles's heart was doing. Martha stood in the aisle, arms folded over her chest, directly in Charles's line of sight, behind and to the right of the pacing Carl Jacks, like she was trying to will Charles to do the right thing.

"We don't want your business, warm or cold," Charles said.

"Okay, . . . *faggot*," Carl said, smiling. He relaxed like he did right before he punched the coach. "Duck, Charles," I yelled, and he lowered his head. Carl caught Charles above the right ear. "Shit," Carl said, "shit, shit, shit," shaking his hand in pain. He'd crunched it against Charles's hard skull. Carl reached for the bottles with his good hand, but Charles quickly snatched them off the counter and placed them on a shelf behind him. Blood trickled from behind his ear.

I felt like I was still trapped in the cooler. "I'm getting out of here," I said. "I quit!" I ran out the door and all the way home. It was early spring, and the cold March air buried itself in my chest. I'd left my jacket behind, and I was still wearing my work apron, but I didn't care. They couldn't do that to me—either of them.

Maybe I should have rejoiced at Charles standing up to Carl Jacks, or worried about his injury, but I only thought of myself— the possibility of getting my own ass kicked. Quitting might save me, I told myself. I wanted the simple life of that photograph above the lunch meat and cheese, two old people in aprons surrounded by the clutter of their small store, satisfied and proud. Like I told Jeanette, I didn't want to kiss anybody else.

You wouldn't think it'd be that big a deal, whether you keep somebody's cheap wine cold or not. That's one of the things I was beginning to learn—that the big things were in the little things. Carl never did kick my ass, but it's not something I'm proud of. By the time his broken hand healed, he'd probably found another store to keep it cold for him. After all, he was old enough to get it anywhere. For all he knew, I quit in support of his need for cold Mad Dog.

I never asked about what happened after I left that night, but I do know that Carl never came in the store again. I know, because after a couple of sleepless weeks, I got up enough nerve and walked in the Jolly Giant early one Saturday morning to apologize, and, like the best families, they took me back.

Middle of the Mitten

Avery didn't know what to make of recent developments. He loved being with Dawn, who wasn't interested in sex at all, and he was seeing Karen, the Snake Lady, who was *only* interested in sex. Neither of them gave a shit about the existence of the other, *so what's the big problem, Avery?* He didn't know. He just didn't know.

The sun sparkled off new snow, and Avery wanted to go outside, hoping the clear dazzle of the day would rub off on him. He threw on his down jacket, snapped the leash on his dog, Max, and headed out the door. He'd named Max after his best friend who had died drinking liquid fertilizer the week after high school graduation back in Detroit. The story went that he'd been cutting grass and was really thirsty and just guzzled the stuff without thinking. Who dreamed that up? It seemed too creative for Max's parents—his father, the droning deacon at the church, and his mother, chief Handmaiden of the Altar. Avery knew Max had killed himself.

Three years later, after his high-school-true-love Debi had dumped him right at the start of his senior year at Alba College, Avery had considered killing himself too. After rattling a handful of pills in his hand for a few hours, he tossed them out the third-floor window of his dorm room. Somebody down on the sidewalk below shouted, "What the fuck was that?"

"Nuclear fallout," he shouted, and slammed the window shut.

A month later, he moved out of the dorm into a tiny off-campus house with his burnout friend, Larry, and shortly after that, he drove to the Animal Rescue League and picked out a mangy little pup. He thought Max would've loved the idea of having a dog named after him—a little twisted, but with feeling behind it.

Max the dog was now taking a large dump in front of Professor Cornwall's house on the corner, despite Avery yanking on the leash and pleading, hissing, "Max, c'mon, let's go!" Cornwall was teaching the astronomy class Avery needed to graduate. Avery glanced at the windows and hoped nobody was looking out.

"When you gotta go, you gotta go." Avery whirled to see Professor Cornwall, briefcase in hand, standing on the sidewalk behind him. He looked more like an old door-to-door insurance salesman than a professor standing in front of his own house.

"I'll clean it up, I promise," Avery sputtered, yanking again, though Max's big feet were firmly planted as he squatted.

"Don't worry, lad. It's just some shit, not spilled milk." Cornwall turned and hurried up his driveway without another word. Intent on making a sale, Avery thought.

Alba was a small college in the "Middle of the Mitten," the lower peninsula of Michigan. It was smaller than Avery's high school back in Detroit. He had chosen it to get as far away from his high school life as possible, hoping to escape Max's ghost, hoping to recreate himself in that small, manageable world—what could be safer than the middle of a mitten?

Avery had taken astronomy thinking it'd have something to do with learning constellations. He imagined impressing women on clear dark nights around the keg at some party, "Now that's Cassiopeia.

And that, that's Gidra the Three-Headed Monster . . ." All he knew were the Dippers, and finding the little one was always tough.

Max was finally done. Happily wagging his tail, he willingly moved on now, pulling Avery forward, straining at the leash. Astronomy turned out to be all math. How far to the stars? Physics in disguise. Avery was failing. Where was Gidra when you needed him? Where was his dead friend, Max? How far away was he?

■ ■ ■

The Snake Lady, that's what everyone called Karen. She had a reputation as a wild woman, and when she invited Avery into her dorm room after a party and unzipped her powder-blue jumpsuit, he was a lost cause. No one had ever made the first move on him, and Avery hadn't made too many first moves himself. He didn't count Debi. He had decided not to date anyone else whose name ended with an "i" and who drew a cute circle to dot it, though he was dismayed to find out how many beautiful women did this.

Later that night, while Avery was puzzling over another chapter in his impossibly thick astronomy textbook, Karen called him at the house. "This is the Snake Lady," she said. "I want a snack." He nearly fainted. "I'll be right over," he managed, then hung up.

"Larry," he shouted. "She calls *herself* the Snake Lady!"

"No way," Larry said, looking up from the kitchen table where he was rolling a joint of his weak homegrown. Avery rushed out of the house and down the street to her dorm.

Karen had one of the few singles on campus. She also was engaged to Todd, an enormous left tackle at another university three hours away. Before Avery had a chance to knock, she opened the door and yanked him in by his scarf. She was already naked. She grabbed his jacket and ripped open all the snaps. He quickly undressed. As he bent to join her in bed, he nodded toward Todd's picture on the nightstand next to the bed.

"You think you could put that away?"

She shrugged. "See you later, Todd," she said, quickly slipping the picture into a drawer and pulling Avery down on top of her.

He held back for a moment. "Let's not try anything new today," he said. Karen had a stack of books and magazines on sexual variations. It was like a class she was studying for—cramming, it felt like to Avery. Brightly colored condoms lined the nightstand like highlighters.

She sighed. "Okay, but I'll have big plans for next time."

Avery fell into her with an urgency that was not love, he knew. But was it even lust? He closed his eyes and held her tight. Afterward, he wanted to talk, to linger.

"Why isn't Todd enough?" he asked as they dressed.

"You're getting a little nosy. Why isn't *this* enough?" She lifted her slit skirt. "I don't ask you what you do when we're not together."

Avery bent to tie his shoes. "Maybe you should ask me. I'd tell you anything."

"Hey, you're not falling in love with me, are you?" she asked.

"No. Don't worry about that," he said. "I've just never had this kind of—whatever it is—before."

She grabbed his hands and pulled him up off the bed.

"I've got to study," she said. "And Todd might be calling soon."

Avery shrugged. "Say 'hi' to Todd for me." He walked out the door, down the hallway, and back out into the cold.

■ ■ ■

"I'm beginning to feel like a sex object," he told Larry.

"No way," Larry said, inhaling deeply.

The last time, he'd had trouble getting hard, even after she'd said, "Tonight, I'm going to take your pants off with my teeth." Maybe it had taken her too long, despite how sexy it had sounded. He'd never had that problem before. Give the Snake Lady credit, he thought, she'd been patient, and he'd responded. *But still,* he said to himself.

"Walk your dog," Larry said. "Look at him—he's bored." Avery looked down at Max, who looked up like a neglected friend. Loose, wrinkled skin folded above his eyes in mournful disappointment. Avery felt guilty about his ordinary life. He missed his dead friend. Larry at best was an interested observer compared to his intimate friendship with Max, who cared, really cared, what Avery thought. And Avery thought a lot back then. Deep, serious thoughts about God and Life and Death and Good and Evil. What happened when you died? How did telephones and TVs squeeze voices and pictures through those wires? Now, Avery only talked like that when he was stoned.

"Okay," he said. "Let's go, Max."

The dog leaped up, then scrabbled over the linoleum, trying to get his footing. Avery took the leash down from the hook. He felt like he was scrabbling too.

"Here, this time I'll wear the collar and you hold the leash, okay?" Avery said, holding the leash out to Max. Larry snorted a laugh. Max just wagged and panted.

Her name was Karen, simply Karen, and Avery thought he'd better start calling her that, and that maybe they should just go to a movie together or something, or maybe just forget the whole thing. Outside, he yanked Max away from the direction of Cornwall's house. Inevitably, if they headed that way, Max stopped in the middle of his lawn and took care of business. It was his favorite spot.

■ ■ ■

"I think Cornwall's getting senile," Avery said to Dawn. She'd taken the course for the same reason Avery had, thinking it'd be an easy science credit.

"He thinks I'm Sheila," Dawn said. "But that's okay. Sheila's smart. Maybe he'll mix up our grades."

Avery smiled. Dawn made him smile. Dawn hated her name.

"My parents say they were hippies," she'd said, "as if that excused everything. I mean, *Dawn,*" she said, stretching it out into two syllables. "People hear that, and they think I like pets and smiley faces and that I put out."

Dawn didn't like pets or smiley faces. She didn't put out. "I don't believe in sex," she told Avery yet again. "Too sweaty."

"Bullshit," Avery said. "Have you tried it?"

"Hey, I tried it. I tried it with guys, I tried it with girls. I just didn't like it."

You could talk in Cornwall's class—he was nearly deaf. He read his lectures verbatim from old, frayed sheets of legal paper, droning on and on, and he wrote on the board so slow it was like he was carving the Ten Commandments.

"Really?" Avery said loudly. "You tried it with girls?"

Heads turned. Dawn looked around the room and gave an exaggerated smile, then she turned back to Avery. "Would I lie about a thing like that?"

"How was it?" Avery asked, lowering his voice. "I've never known any lesbians."

"Don't be an idiot, Av, you've known plenty . . . Though I am not a lesbian. They sweat like everybody else."

Avery shrugged. "I like sweating." He also liked when she called him "Av." No one had ever called him that except Max. Whenever she called him Av, it was like a tiny tender seed sprouted inside him.

He had given her detailed descriptions of his encounters with the Snake Lady, and Dawn seemed both incredulous and interested.

Up in the front of the lecture hall, Cornwall was cleaning his glasses with the cleaning fluid and cloth that he kept in his breast pocket at all times.

"I can't believe she just has sex with you like it's . . . it's a doctor's appointment or something. I'd like to see that . . . Maybe I could watch sometime—it doesn't sound like your friend would mind."

Avery made a choking noise, and everyone looked at him, even Cornwall.

"Are you okay, young man?" he asked, putting his glasses back on and peering up at Avery. "Aren't you the one with the poopy dog?"

The class roared with laughter. *The one with the poopy dog.* He could see it under his photo in the yearbook. His face, already flushed by Dawn's statement, now turned an even deeper red, an overripe tomato ready to split with humiliation. "Yes, I'm okay," Avery shouted, then he bent down and pretended to take notes as Cornwall found his place and continued the lecture.

Dawn passed him a note: "I still love you, even if you do have a poopy dog." She had written *still* as if she had loved him for some time. He slipped the note in his pocket and smiled at her. It was something to keep. He was starting to feel like he truly did love Dawn. That old tag line, "like a friend," sounded woefully inadequate compared to what he felt. As he lay in bed alone at nights, he replayed their conversations. She made him laugh. She made him think. She let him talk about the little people inside TV sets.

Dawn was petite, with blonde hair, blue eyes. More of a "Dawn" than she ever wanted to be. She cut her hair short at a severe angle, but it just revealed a beautiful neck that Avery found himself staring at in class.

■ ■ ■

"I want to kiss your neck," he told her one day after class as they sat at what had become *their* table in the Student Union.

"Go ahead," she said.

"Right here?"

"Sure."

Avery looked around. No one was paying attention to them, as usual. He bent over and slowly put his lips on the sweet spot where shoulder met neck. He closed his eyes and rested his lips there. He opened his mouth slightly and gave her his best kiss, slow and careful.

"That's enough," she said. He lifted his head and studied her carefully. Did she look aroused? Her thin smile revealed nothing.

"Did you feel anything just now?" he asked.

"Does the pope wear high heels?"

"Maybe. He might . . ." Avery drifted into silence, closing his eyes, thinking about that kiss.

"Yesterday I felt like I was going to fall into the sky," she said. Avery opened his eyes. She was looking away from him and out the window at thick, gray clouds.

"If you did that, would you be falling up or down?"

"Let's ask Cornwall."

■ ■ ■

"My friend Dawn asked if she could watch us sometime. Isn't that crazy?" Avery was pulling up his jeans. Karen was pulling up hers.

She stopped. "Watch? What's so crazy about that? What do you think pornography's all about?"

Avery lost his balance and tumbled to the floor. "Yeah, but *in person.* That's pretty kinky," he said, looking up at her. "I mean . . . I don't know."

"The pressure, yeah," she said, laughing. "I don't think you could handle it."

"What do you mean?" Avery gave the laugh he gave whenever he felt threatened—high-pitched and loud, more like a squeak.

"You seem pretty tense lately. You were relaxed when we first started this."

This. Avery hated when she talked like that. What should they call *this?* Foolishness, probably. Karen was premed with nearly a 4.0. That's because she doesn't waste time getting emotional, Avery thought—at least not with me. He shook his head and got to his feet.

"For one thing," Karen said, "I can't believe she doesn't enjoy sex. There's good sex and there's lousy sex. There isn't *no* sex. She's just hiding behind something. She's afraid . . . Bring her along next time—if she's serious."

Avery yanked on his boots. "Does Todd know about *this?*" He knew she saw her boyfriend every weekend.

She shook her head. "He wouldn't understand."

"So," Avery said, "*he* wouldn't want to watch then, would he?"

She looked at her watch. "He'll be calling soon. You'd better get going."

■ ■ ■

There was no getting around it—Avery was failing astronomy. Dawn was getting a C, but Avery was failing.

Dawn wasn't a classic beauty. Neither was Avery. Her nose was long and a little hooked. Her eyes seemed too far apart. She didn't have much of a butt. These were all things she told him one afternoon in the Union, and Avery agreed. "We don't have to bullshit about things like that," Dawn said. Avery told her his ears were too big, that he was already getting a little gut, and that his hair was greasy. Dawn nodded.

"Can we get married now?" he asked her. "I need someone to support me—I can't graduate without passing astronomy."

"Okay," Dawn said. "You'll have to cook and clean house . . . and get rid of the poopy dog."

Max had eaten two of Larry's sci-fi paperbacks last week, and Avery had halfheartedly smacked the dog's butt with a newspaper a few times in an attempt at discipline.

"The dog was a mistake. Is a mistake," Avery admitted.

"Better than killing yourself, I suppose," Dawn said. Avery suddenly felt tired and sad. He remembered how he and Max had blown up the chem lab in high school and had gotten suspended. They'd been trying to make a bomb.

"I'd never kill myself," Avery said.

"Good," she said. She surprised him then by touching the side of his face. "I don't want to be a widow."

"Why don't we try sex just once and see what happens? Why don't you give it another whirl?"

"Another whirl. What is a whirl? I know what a twirl is, but what's a whirl? Anyway, what do you need sex from me for when you've got your friend."

"She's not my friend," Avery said, surprising himself. Though it was true. They weren't friends, and Avery was thinking the unthinkable. He was thinking of giving up sex—sex with the Snake Lady.

"I'm getting tired of it. Maybe I'll join you in the nunnery."

"You just said you wanted us to try it, now you say you're tired of it. Sounds like great fun."

He almost said, "I want to try it with *you*." But she knew that. He was beginning to think, despite all the long discussions with his dead friend Max, that he did indeed have a soul. Something inside him ached all the time these days, and it wasn't another ulcer, like the one he had after Max died and he drank endless cups of coffee and stopped sleeping because sleep was like death.

Avery was drinking too much coffee again. Beneath the table, his legs twitched. "She said you could come and watch if you wanted."

"Really?"

"Yeah. She doesn't care. She's something else."

They both fell silent. Their Styrofoam cups were empty. Avery had broken his into a small pile of pieces, which he scooped up and dropped in Dawn's cup.

"Shoveling the snow," Avery said finally. Outside, it was deep. More on the way. Maybe some kind of record. Their small school never closed. No one had to go far for anything.

"Av, you've got a good mind. It's just not made for physics. Neither is mine." Avery felt like she'd just admitted something. Like she'd just said she didn't want to watch. It'd been a game to see who'd say it first. He knew it was an impossibility. He couldn't even picture the three of them alone in a room together fully clothed, much less naked.

"Time to check on Max," he said. He rose and began walking to the door, then turned back to her suddenly. "Whirl is just a fancy word for twirl," he said. "Why don't we give it a twirl?"

She cupped her hands under her mouth and blew air toward him.

"Hey, is that some obscene gesture I don't know about?" he asked.

"I'm just blowing you a hug," she said.

■　■　■

The snow was so deep Avery had to walk in the middle of the plowed street to get home. His could barely lift his feet as he trudged over the high snowbank where the sidewalk used to be. Max would need a walk in this. Avery groaned. Just his luck to fall in love with someone who doesn't like sex. Who *thinks* she doesn't like sex, he told himself.

"Just your luck to have the Snake Lady," Larry had said that morning.

"Don't call her that," Avery said.

"Why not? Snake lost its charms?" Larry leered.

"I have looked the gift horse in the mouth," Avery said, "and now . . ." He didn't finish. And now, what? He couldn't finish his thoughts, his sentences, his astronomy homework.

When he finally arrived home, there was a message to call Karen. Max was circling at his feet. He dialed her number from memory. They'd been together maybe a dozen times over the past two months.

"Are you up for a visit?" she asked.

Avery hesitated. He still had his boots on—they were melting snow onto the dirty kitchen linoleum. Larry was lighting up a bowl. He motioned to Avery. Avery shook his head *no*.

"Are you there?" she asked.

"More or less," he said. "I have to take my dog for a walk in this snow."

"The poopy dog," she laughed harshly. Avery felt like she was ready to cross him off the list, look for another "backdoor man," as she called him.

"It's good to hear you laugh," he said. "Hey, why don't you come *here?*"

"What's the matter?" she asked.

"There's two feet of snow on the ground."

"Yeah, and you want *me* to walk over *there?*"

"Hey, it's something new to try."

Avery was never good with the telephone. He felt like he had a black rock in his hand. He could never handle the disembodied voice without a face to read. His own voice was a low rumble that made most people ask, no matter what time of day or night, whether they'd woken him up. His usual conversation lasted thirty seconds. He'd say anything to get off the phone.

"I'll be right over," he said.

He opened his backpack and handed Larry replacements for the eaten books to lighten his load before he headed out. Larry squinted up at him and smiled.

"Cool," he said. "Your dog has good taste in books."

It was always "your dog." Not "Max," not "the dog," not "our dog." Living with Larry was not the fun Avery had imagined it would be. Larry's stoned-out comments didn't seem so funny on a daily basis. It was still better than that little box of a room he'd shared with Jeremiah Pugh, "the roommate nobody wanted." His previous roommate, Doug, who was a nice enough guy, had pulled a double switch and dumped Jeremiah on Avery to help out his own friend who'd been stuck with him. Jeremiah was a born-again folk singer with alcoholic parents. He ended up having a nervous break-down, which left Avery with a single for two months, then he either had to pay the price for a single or accept whatever roommate the university dumped on him.

Avery himself was not a good roommate. He didn't like other people watching him sleep. He didn't sleep. He didn't allow his roommates to sleep. He had gone through five of them until finally getting permission to live off campus. He'd won the battle of the bad roommates with Jeremiah, but had taken no pride in that. He'd admired Jeremiah for believing in something so intensely. But, unlike his old friend Max, Jeremiah would not entertain alternate views, so they'd lapsed into a tense silence, broken only by Jeremiah's off-key singing. Then one day, Jeremiah walked out of the room in his bathrobe, guitar around his neck, and wandered the streets singing until someone gave him a ride to the state hospital. He'd been writing Avery letters. Jeremiah had told Avery about sin eaters, so he tried to feed the letters to Max, believing that might make Jeremiah well, but he just sniffed them and walked away.

■　■　■

Avery showed up at Karen's dorm room with Max on the leash.

She opened the door and yanked them both in, frowning. "What's with the dog?"

"He wants to watch," Avery said. She punched him hard in the arm, but then immediately began stripping off his layers of winter clothes. He realized he could say whatever mean thing he wanted to her—it had no effect, as long as he performed. "Just make sure he's quiet," she said as she struggled with his buttons.

"Max," Avery said. "Lay down." Max wagged his tail excitedly and turned in circles in the tiny room. "He'll settle down," Avery said hopefully. But he did not settle down. "He likes a good book," Avery said. She didn't laugh.

Avery was lying on his back, Karen riding him, when Max suddenly jumped up on the bed. She hissed at him and shoved him down to the floor. Her eyes were full of concentration and fury. Max was spooked and quickly lay down on the rug in front of the door.

Afterward, as Avery was lacing his boots, someone knocked at the door, then quickly jiggled the knob.

"Hey Karen, it's me." A deep drunken slur vibrated through the door. Avery knew instantly who it was. He was trapped. Max scrambled up and scratched at the door.

"Karen. Karen? What the fuck? You got a dog in there?"

Karen's face paled, highlighting the freckles around her nose. Avery's fingers trembled as he fumbled with his laces. Karen, still naked, sat frozen in place on the bed. Todd was pounding on the door, yelling, "Karen, Karen!"

"Go in the bathroom," Avery whispered. He led her silently inside, handed her some clothes, and shut the door. He turned and walked back to the locked door, took a deep breath, and turned the knob. Todd's neck was as thick as Avery's waist. Avery held Max's leash in his fist. "Hi, you must be Todd. Hi, Todd, I was just doing some homework with Karen, she's in the bathroom she'll be right . . ."

Todd grabbed him around the throat and punched him in the left eye. Avery's head rocked back. Max jumped on Todd, distracting him while Avery wriggled free. The leash wrapped itself around Todd's feet, and he tripped trying to chase Avery, who staggered down the hall and out the door. Max pulled himself loose and ran after him. Todd followed them outside into the deep drifts. He started out gaining on Avery, but like a rhino, his charge was limited, and after about fifty yards Avery began lengthening the distance between them. His eye was quickly swelling shut. Max was in front of him now—he knew the way home.

After about a quarter-mile, Todd stopped and bent at the waist. He was spitting or puking or just catching his breath—Avery couldn't tell as he glanced back. His throat burned cold as he gasped for air, but he kept on clomping down the icy street. The high piles of snow on either side of the road made Avery feel as if he was running down a tunnel. He remembered that people with near-death experiences said it was like going down a long white tunnel.

He laughed, despite the pain. It was an irony Max would have loved. Max the dog was beginning to limp, ice wedging itself into his paws. He lay down and started biting at it. Max was a big dog, part lab, part shepherd, but Avery picked him up and carried him the rest of the way home. When they stumbled in the door, Larry looked at them and shook his head, hummed a sympathetic reproach. Avery tried to steady himself, leaning hard against the wall and gripping the top of a kitchen chair. He was thawing out into pain.

"We should put a steak on that eye or something," Larry said.

They both laughed—they could never afford steak—though Avery felt like crying. Larry pulled a pound of hamburger out of the fridge and handed it over. Avery held it against his eye. The cold felt good, but the burger was already thawed, and the package began leaking blood onto Avery's face, making him look even more of a mess. He gave up and unwrapped the burger, putting it in Max's bowl. Max quickly gobbled it up. Larry didn't ask any questions, and Avery was grateful.

■ ■ ■

Dawn. Avery needed to talk to Dawn. Max was sleeping off his burger. Midnight, but he knew Dawn would be up. She lived off campus too, in a tiny third-floor apartment on the next block. Larry was listening to music on his headphones when Avery slipped out the door.

He walked up the back stairs to her apartment and knocked softy. Dawn immediately swung open the door and took him in her arms.

"The boyfriend," Avery said. "He didn't want to watch." She sighed deeply. "Oh, Av, you're such an asshole," she said with such tenderness and warmth that he collapsed completely against her, and she had to take a step backward for balance.

He wanted to say something clever like "My poopy dog saved my life," or "I finally saw stars," but he couldn't say anything just now in her warm embrace. She looked at him again and gently touched his swollen eye. She put her lips to it.

The snowstorm had ended. The sky was clear and black, and a half-moon shone a good, kind light down on the snow as they walked out into it. In an empty field by the railroad tracks, they fell back into the deep, untouched snow. It was one of those nights where the whole world seemed to tilt and you suddenly could tell whatever secrets you had. One of those nights where a half-moon was plenty.

"Why do you think your friend Max killed himself?" she asked.

"I've got a long list of reasons. Sometimes I add new things to the list. Sometimes I cross out reasons . . .

"You know, Max and I, we . . ." Avery paused. "Max and I tried it . . . just boys checking things out, I guess. He'd wanted to do it again, but it seemed kind of creepy to me."

"You think he loved you, like that?"

"Oh, I don't know. That's one of the things that goes on and off the list. We were going away to different colleges. That bothered him. Bothered me too. I didn't know he was going to the College of No Return. A little secret he was keeping from me." Avery felt a tear sliding off his cheek into the snow.

They lay together for long minutes. Every sound was cushioned by snow. "When I was a kid," she began, "eight or nine." She stopped. Avery waited. "My grandfather was dying. He lived across the street from us. One day I brought him his lunch in bed, and he asked me to come close. I stood beside him and he reached over and undid my pants and pulled them down and pulled my underwear down, and then he touched me. Afterward, he said, 'Don't ever let anyone touch you like that.' "

Avery twisted his head in the snow and tried to see her face. She was staring straight up.

"I've got a list," she said, "of reasons he might've done something like that. Sometimes I wonder if I dreamt the whole thing. I mean, other than that, I just remember this sweet, loving man. So, I think, well, why didn't he just *tell* me that. Why did he have to touch me?"

Avery didn't know what to say. He reached out and took her gloved hand in his. The snow was melting through his clothes, but it felt good packed against his swollen eye.

"I feel like he put some kind of curse on me," she blurted out and squeezed his hand tightly. Even through the thick gloves, he felt it.

"I'm sorry," Avery said. "I'm sorry."

"That's what we say when there's nothing else to say," Dawn said.

"Yes," said Avery, "I'm sorry. I'm sorry I said I'm sorry."

She laughed. "It gets confusing."

"It doesn't *get* confusing. It *is* confusing," Avery said. He almost felt like he was talking to Max. They fell into a comfortable silence.

"You know," said Avery finally, "I really don't want to know how far away the stars are. I just like them real small, the way they are. I just like them up there, all twinkly and everything."

"All twinkly and everything," Dawn repeated.

"There's the Big Dipper," Avery said.

"There's the Little Dipper," Dawn said.

"That means we both pass," Avery said.

"That means we both get As," Dawn said.

"Let's not be greedy," Avery said.

"No, let's be greedy," Dawn said.

"Okay, let's," Avery said. In the deep, pure snow, he felt like nothing could harm them. "Hey, you want to make angels?" he asked.

"No," she said, "I don't believe in them."

"Me neither," he said. He got up on his elbow and turned to kiss her, but she rolled over on top of him, her body pressing him deeper through the snow. He wrapped his arms around her, and they held each other down.

Cross Country

We figured we'd drive to California—unusual for Detroit boys. Why go to California when Florida was closer? Beaches and palm trees. Palm trees and beaches. I wasn't sure why California myself, but Jimmy was all hot for it. He'd read this book called *On the Road.* Whenever I tell anyone here in New York about the trip, they say, "Oh, like *On the Road.*" Now, I know it's one of America's great clichés, but then we were just a couple of nineteen-year-old factory rats.

I never much expected to do anything new or original in this life, but at the time we felt we were going on a great, unique adventure, and that counts for something—feeling that way—regardless of the facts. One thing about our country, it's still pretty big, no matter how small everybody says it's getting. When we got in Jimmy's stupid little Gremlin that hot, August morning, I could almost feel the world opening up for us, could almost smell the newness in the air. Like cartoon dogs lifted up by the scent of food, we were floating toward it.

We had a cooler full of beer and cans of this spray cheese Jimmy was hooked on, along with some crackers, though after a few beers, Jimmy just sprayed that cheese right in his mouth. We'd both been working at the Chrysler plant down on Mound Road for nearly a year, then we'd gotten laid off. All through high school, we'd been counting on those jobs, but they just disappeared—poof—and we had no idea what to do next.

I'm writing this because Jimmy is dead, and now that I know a few people who died, it bothers me, how they can just disappear, life going on as if they never existed. We're all just specks of dust somebody's going to sweep up someday, and there's always more dust coming along behind. His girlfriend, Shell—Michelle—I could not believe how fast she up and married our pal Sal. The other thing is, we can't control how people are going to remember us. Here's the story about my trip with Jimmy. I like to hold it tight to my chest, to curl around it when everything starts pushing in on me.

After spending a lot of time in a car with somebody, you start to notice their irritating little quirks. Jimmy plucked hairs out of his scraggly beard. It's a wonder he had any beard left, the way he'd single out a hair and yank it, one after another. It hurt just to watch, but he never winced. He probably wasn't even conscious of doing it. I think he was numbed by all the pain he'd already experienced. His father had died of a heart attack when we were freshmen in high school. Two years later, his younger brother committed suicide after this total loser of a girl dumped him. Jimmy never understood that kind of thinking—he never looked back, except on this trip.

I was secretly in love with his older sister, Jacqueline. Jackie. It made me guilty about being friends with Jimmy, and a little scared to be attracted to that cursed family. I wondered if something was wrong with their house, though it looked like all the others on our straight, flat street of assembly-line houses. My nickname was EJ (my initials—nothing very imaginative) but Jimmy's mother was the only adult who called me EJ. Everybody else called me Ed, Eddie, or, worse, Edward. "Hey EJ!" she used to say when I walked in the door. Theirs was a house you could just walk in—they didn't stand on ceremony. I was always hoping to see Jackie in some state of undress, and from time to time I did. She never seemed to give a shit, and that made me love her even more.

In my family, everybody wore pajamas and robes. It was like my father wanted to keep our house completely orderly and civilized because the factory where he spent most of his days was such a zoo. One time when we were kids, Jimmy came over to spend the night, and my mom told us to get ready for bed, so Jimmy and I went in my room and I put on my pj's, but Jimmy just stripped to his underwear and went back into the living room. My mother nearly fainted.

A few years after his dad died, Jimmy's mom, Stella, started seeing other men, but they all seemed intimidated by the atmosphere in that house. You never saw the same guy more than a couple of times, but if Jimmy's mom was disappointed, she never let on. "Hey EJ!"—and the way she made grilled cheese sandwiches—she stuck three of those plastic slices of American cheese on each sandwich. Three! The cheese just oozed out between the bread. I guess when you lose a husband and a son, what's another slice of cheese? Maybe that's why Jimmy liked the spray cheese—the mess of it. Nothing in life is as bland or predictable as one slice of American cheese.

Jimmy was one of those guys who'd always be called Jimmy, even if he'd lived to be an old man. He was a joker—a live wire. It was like he was trying to make up for the others dying by being more alive. One year, he let a terrified turkey loose in the hallway of our high school the day before Thanksgiving. Sometimes it seemed like he was trying too hard, but he was always trying.

My mother says I romanticize this trip, and maybe she's right, but I think she's a little jealous, particularly with Jimmy dead (it was just a stupid car accident—he wasn't even drunk—somebody trying to pass on a two-laner wiped him out coming the other way). She says I've made him some kind of legend. You decide for yourself. Do legends pick their beards like that? Well, okay. Okay, the poor guy's dead—let me at least make him a little bit legendary. Maybe it'll make *you* remember him. That tiny gravestone sure isn't going to catch anybody's eye.

We spent the second night on the road near Omaha with my cousin Eric. A little older than us, he had his own place and worked as a waiter at a fancy restaurant. He showed us Omaha's nightlife—lousy cover bands and cheap drinks, just like home. He liked Jimmy instantly—most people did. The next morning, bleary-eyed, we headed out his door to the car.

"Why don't you guys just stay out here?" Eric asked. "I could probably get you jobs. Ever wait tables before?"

Jimmy and I looked at each other.

"Jimmy, you got the personality for it," he said. "EJ, well—we'd need to do some work on you."

We all laughed. "I'm more of a dishwasher type," I said. "I got experience at that."

Jimmy was quiet, thinking. "Well," he said, "we'll stop on our way back. Who knows. I'm too hung over to think. Who's driving?"

"I finished yesterday. I think it's your turn," I said.

Jimmy sighed. "I guess if I put on my radar shades, I'll be okay . . ." We got in, waved to Eric, gently slammed the doors, and pulled away.

Jimmy had a pair of wraparound sunglasses that had belonged to his father, and he thought they were magic. He claimed they helped him detect police cars across great distances. All I know is that they made him look like a punk. Jimmy's dad was thirty-six when he died. He wasn't overweight or anything—some defect had gone undetected. I think everybody's got defects that go undetected. Sometimes they kill you, sometimes they make you an asshole.

Jackie and her mom still live in that house back on the edge of Detroit. Jackie got married and divorced, then moved back home with her son. I have dinner there when I'm in town. My family thinks that's a little weird, but it's part of how I remember Jimmy. It's good to go someplace where somebody still calls me EJ. In New York, I'm a definite Edward.

Jimmy drove a Gremlin because one of his uncles sold it to him cheap—rusting out, but low mileage. Its tiny, four-liter engine struggled through the Rockies. "C'mon," we'd say, rocking back and forth in our seats to get up the mountains. It overheated once, and we had to stop. We stood next to the car and took pictures of each other with our arms spread wide as if to say, "Look at us—look at all this," goofy grins on our faces, snow-covered mountains behind us. We weren't big enough to take it all in. It seemed like those mountains were bigger than our imaginations. We hadn't even thought about them when we started the trip—we'd just thought of Las Vegas, and California beaches, beautiful women, parties. Nothing real.

We were both trying to figure out what to do next. Jimmy wanted to get into sports broadcasting, but he didn't know how. The radio advertised the Specs Howard School of Broadcasting, but the ads for it were so horrible, we couldn't imagine you'd learn anything there. "Specs Howard?" Jimmy would say incredulously. " 'Specs?' Do they hand out nicknames for you there? Does Specs look at you and say, 'you're Boomer,' 'you're Big Red'? I bet they fight over 'Madman.' Maybe I'll just skip the other stuff and start my own broadcasting school . . . Who the hell *is* Specs Howard, that's what I want to know."

"There sure are a lot of Madmen out there."

"Jumpin' Jimmy," he said under his breath.

I found out later that Jimmy had looked into Specs's school, but the tuition was high, and he couldn't get a loan just for broadcasting school. I had set my sights lower and was looking into bartending school. "I think I've drunk enough to know some of that shit already," I told Jimmy, and we both laughed. It was called the International School of Bartending—maybe to attract some Canadians from across the border.

We switched to pop that day. The dry air and heat and hangovers cracked our lips. We guzzled Coke after Coke. "Hey, we should make a commercial out of this," Jimmy said. He jotted it down on his idea pad he kept in the car. I always felt hopeful about Jimmy's future. No one else I knew kept an idea pad.

"Would you work in the plant again if they called us back?"

"No, I wouldn't go back," I said. I kept changing my mind. We debated it daily. "It was making me crazy anyway—the same thing all day, every day. I don't know how my dad stands it," I said. "He doesn't get high or nothing. He just comes home every day like it's no big deal. When I'm a bartender, there'll be new people every day. Always something new."

"Yeah," Jimmy said. "And broadcasting too. I mean, every day, new games. Interviewing the players, doing play-by-play."

"The money in the plant though—you can't beat it," I said.

"That's the thing," Jimmy said. We were running out of unemployment in three weeks. We were supposed to come back from our trip with evidence of having looked for work, but with our benefits running out so soon, it hardly seemed worth the effort.

"That's the thing," he said again, and yanked another hair out of his beard.

We fell into the silence of the road hum, the blur of wind through the open windows. No music. That day, we stopped listening to all the tapes we'd made for the trip. What seemed clever back home was now making us groan and push the fast-forward button. Our third day on the road, and we were already running out of gas.

"I might go back. But it ain't gonna happen—they're not gonna call us back—those jobs are long gone," I said, half-relieved, half-scared. Jimmy and I had been on different shifts, and we'd rarely seen each other since we'd started at the plant. Until we were laid off, it was beginning to seem like our friendship had been a thing of childhood, adolescence. Jimmy was on midnights, and I was on afternoons, three to eleven. It was tough finding anybody to hang out with when I was off, except the other afternoon guys. I'd sit with them in the bars till closing time, then go home and sleep.

Since the layoffs, we'd started hanging around together again, drinking too much, just like in high school. We'd even gone to a couple of high school parties looking for girls, though our status as laid off factory workers didn't help us any. Those guys in school could still pretend they were going to do big things, but it was pretty clear that, for the moment, we were not. But we were happy just hanging out together again. It was like one of us had moved away, then moved back.

"I don't know," Jimmy said. "If I could find another job paying that kind of money . . ."

We were just shooting the shit like that when an unmarked police car stopped us. It was the goofiest thing—the cops didn't even have radar. They were dressed in softball uniforms, and one of them stuck a little flashing light on the roof as they pulled us over.

Jimmy had been close to his brother Clete. They fought in the way that brothers fought, vicious and full of love. Clete tagged along behind us. I can still hear him yelling, "Hey, wait up, you guys!" We always waited, Jimmy throwing his hands up and frowning, smacking his brother on the arm when he finally caught up.

When Clete killed himself, Jimmy found him. He yanked him out of the car and tried to get him breathing again, pounding on his chest, but he was long gone. I stuck with Jimmy and the family all through the funeral, Jimmy crying and wiping snot on my shirt. His mother and sister talked about Clete sometimes, but Jimmy never said a word to me about his dead brother, and I wasn't asking.

When somebody that young dies, usually the family either obliterates all traces, or leaves the kid's things exactly as they were. Jimmy's mom did something in between. The house was too small for a shrine to anyone. They'd already gone through it all with his father. You'd find traces of Clete everywhere—his baseball glove, his bike in the garage, an old T-shirt turned into a rag. I didn't know how Clete's death affected Jimmy until that trip, but it's all that could explain our turning around in the middle of Utah, and how Jimmy hugged his mother and sister hard, for long minutes upon our return, both of them looking at me and shrugging, Jackie giggling.

"Oh shit," Jimmy said, which I guess is what everybody says when a cop pulls them over, softball uniform or not. "What do we do with the pot?"

It was in the glove box. "Leave it and pray," I said. They were already getting out of their car and heading toward us. One of them clearly wasn't interested. He held back, hoping, I think, that his partner would say, "to hell with it," and let us go so they could get to their game. Jimmy took off his radar shades and gently set them on the dashboard. He knew the importance of seeing someone's eyes.

"Michigan, eh?" the serious cop said after he looked at Jimmy's license. "What brings you boys out here?"

"California," I said.

Jimmy winced as if I'd told an obvious, blatant lie. Maybe hearing it aloud like that made the whole trip suddenly seem silly to him.

"We're just driving around for awhile to try and figure out what we're going to do. We both got laid off from our jobs, so we decided to see the country," he said.

"You're driving too fast to see much of it," the other cop said. "Must be hot in that little thing. You boys can step out if you'd like."

We were both drenched in sweat and quickly slipped out the doors onto the shoulder of the busy freeway.

"We're looking for a campground before it gets dark," Jimmy said.

We stood in the gravel, cars zipping past us, pushing hot breeze and exhaust into our faces.

The cops looked at each other. "There's a campground right near our ball field," Officer Hatch, the less serious one, said. Officer Bradley went back to his car with Jimmy's license to radio it in and check him out.

"You guys got sharp uniforms," Jimmy said. "I like that blue— pretty snazzy. What position you play?"

Hatch smiled ruefully, "Catcher—when I play. I can't run worth a darn . . . Hey, we're gonna be late," he shouted above the traffic to Bradley, pointing to his watch.

"How fast was I going?" Jimmy asked.

"Oh, I don't know," Hatch said. "Ask my partner—this was his idea."

"You follow any of the pro teams?" Jimmy asked.

"Nah," Hatch said, squinting into the setting sun. He was about forty, I guessed—my father's age—and he had a little potbelly. He was short and squat, like you'd expect a catcher to be.

"I have to admit, I don't know much about Utah," Jimmy said.

"Well, you might be learning a bit about our speeding laws in just a minute."

We all laughed. I wanted to pace, but I knew with cops around, you just stood still. I'd gotten into the traveling rhythm and the sudden stop jolted me. Jimmy seemed incredibly comfortable, as if he'd just stopped by to visit some old friends. He had a clean driving record. Bradley handed him back his license and registration and gave him a warning.

"Follow us if you're looking for a campground," Bradley said.

Hatch smiled and shook his head. "He's the star of the team. Thinks they won't start the game without him."

We all got back in our cars, and we followed them to a campground on the edge of a huge softball complex.

"Can you believe that?" I shouted to Jimmy as we pulled out behind them. "High fives!" I shouted, but Jimmy said, "Keep your hands down—I'm driving. I'm sure they're looking in the mirror at us."

"Hey, they're letting us go," I said. "I'd call that lucky. I was beginning to think those sunglasses weren't working." Jimmy left them on the dashboard, and they slid to the floor when we turned off the freeway.

"Leave the sunglasses out of it," Jimmy said.

We pulled up next to the cops when they stopped in the gravel parking lot. Jimmy thanked them for the help and asked what diamond they were playing on. "We'll come over after we set up our tent," he said. "Maybe I'll do the play-by-play. I'm thinking about going into broadcasting."

I stayed at the tent, and Jimmy didn't insist that I join him. I didn't want to go see some Utah state cops play softball. That's not what I was driving to California for, I told myself, though besides getting drunk and stoned, we didn't have much of an agenda. That was supposed to be against the *On the Road* rules, having things mapped out.

I'm sorry now that I didn't go to the game, because when Jimmy came back, he lifted the flap of our little pup tent and said, "Let's just turn around and go home. What are we doing out here anyway?"

"Having fun?" I ventured. "What are you talking about? What are we missing out on back home?"

He'd sat on the bench with Hatch, who never got in the game. Bradley hit three home runs. They didn't go out for beer after the game, like everybody did in Detroit. They stood around by their cars and told stories about their families.

"Sounds like they brainwashed you." I didn't think he was serious about going home. "Did you tell any of your stories?" I asked.

"Nah, I just listened," he said. "Hey, do you talk to your dad much?" he asked. He was slipping into his sleeping bag. I could barely see him in the light from his wandering flashlight.

"No, not much," I said. "You know that."

"Yeah. Yeah, I do," he said. He clicked off the flashlight and fell back with a sigh. The distant lights from the softball field filtered through the thick trees and into our tent.

"You don't really want to go home," I said. "What about Las Vegas tomorrow?"

"I don't have anything to bet on anyway," he said. He could have meant *with*, bet *with*, but I remember *on* so clearly, as if he were just then looking ahead, not to the slot machines and blackjack tables, but to the rest of his life.

I was sure he'd change his mind in the morning, but he got right behind the wheel and started driving back the way we'd came. "I'm not an *On the Road* guy. I'm sorry. I thought I was," Jimmy said. He picked fiercely at his beard.

I turned away and rolled down my window. The car was already heating up. "What are we gonna tell everybody—we turned around in Utah because? Because? I don't get it. I just don't get it."

"Because we felt like it," he said.

"Because *you* felt like it," I replied.

To me, nothing unusual had happened that night. Some decent cops let us off the hook. But Jimmy acted as if he'd been rescued, called back to his mother and sister, his place there.

Broadcasting school might not seem like a big dream to give up, but I think the dreams that are halfway realistic are the hardest ones to relinquish. After all, Jimmy had won a speech contest at school once. He loved sports, and knew all the players, all the teams. And he had the confidence to speak to strangers. But he ended up going to school for copy machine repair, and it paid off with a good-paying job that he had until he died. I don't know what would've come of Jimmy, whether he would have fixed Xerox machines his whole life or what. I don't know how his mother still lives with the ghosts of all those cut-off lives. She still calls me "EJ" with the old affection. I suppose in a family like that, simple survival is dream enough. When I feel myself forgetting Jimmy, I pull a hair out of my own beard and feel the pain.

"You're the closest I've got to a son now," Stella told me once. "Don't say that," Jackie yelled from the bathroom. "They don't let you marry your brother." When she came out, I gave them both a tight squeeze, like Jimmy did when we came back from our trip.

Bartending school had a waiting list of unemployed auto workers, so I went to cooking school instead. The Culinary Institute in New York is the best one in the country, and I did get a loan to go *there.* I had returned with Jimmy to wait for the miracle callback to the plant, only to end up grill cook down at Clem's, a local dive. When Jimmy died, I started keeping my own idea pad. I pumped up a dream and found out it held air. It actually floated. My home is in a kitchen now—the warmth, the pure smells, the wonderful chaos.

"You can't really make yourself over in a new place." I wrote that in my idea pad. Even in New York, where everybody calls me "Edward," I'm still "Jimmy's best friend." Everything you're going to be is already inside you. Jimmy might've figured that out back then. I've never gone to California, though I've had my chances. I told Stella and Jackie that I'm keeping that square empty on my map.

On the way home, we didn't stop to see Eric. We weren't talking much. Turning around and going home without ever making it to California—that just seemed crazy to me. I told Jimmy he was chickening out.

"Chickening out on what?" he asked.

"On everything," I said. "You were Mr. *On the Road*—adventure, getting away, new experiences, all that stuff."

"Chickening out on what?" he asked again, as if he hadn't heard me.

It was his car, and I had no choice. I could have gotten out and hitchhiked the rest of the way—people still did that then—but it would've meant a permanent break with my oldest friend.

Out of nowhere, I said, "Wait up you guys," in a voice I'm sure he recognized as Clete's. It was unforgivable, but it was my answer. Jimmy swung at me and missed, the car swerving toward the shoulder. He grabbed the wheel and swerved back. After that, we hardly spoke for the rest of the trip.

I guess he'd seen what he needed to see, though he never explained it to me in a way that made sense. A lot of us feel like we want to go home, but how often do we do it? How often do we even know what home is? What he did seems brave to me now, not chickening out at all.

I guess there's not much legendary about it, but how many people heading to California stop in Utah, Utah of all places, and turn around? It was a different kind of road for Jimmy. A shorter road. His mother and sister greeted us warmly and without surprise, as if we'd just gone out for a couple of hours. I lingered there through the afternoon, despite being tired and still mad at Jimmy, then I went home to my own family, where I had to explain everything.

Karaoke Moon

"It would've been nice to have some geraniums," Maura said, pulling down her floppy sun hat against the cold wind.

"They all died. The frost killed them. Turned them all to mush," Daniel said, moving his plastic lounge chair away from the large, empty planters where the geraniums were supposed to be. He blew his nose loudly and with great ceremony. "You ever notice when you have a cold and it's really running and you blow your nose like that and it's like your whole head drains? I mean, you can hear again and everything." He paused and sighed.

"What are you talking about?" she asked.

"It feels like taking a good shit, that's what I meant to say," he said. "This cold's got me all muddled up—I don't know if I'm finishing my sentences or just imagining I finish them."

Maura felt like letting the hat blow away, off their hotel balcony and out to sea, but that would be admitting the trip was a total bust. "The brochure promised geraniums," she persisted.

"Well, maybe we can get a dead geranium clause inserted next time," Daniel said. He draped a towel over his bald head.

Maura took off her sunglasses. "You know damn well we're never coming back here."

"Hey, it's not so bad," he said. "I just wish we could get out of the wind. That's the problem with islands. You never think about it when you book these places, but when you get there, there's nothing to stop the wind. It just blows and blows."

"It just blows and blows," she said, "like your nose." Maura was a retired office manager at a medium-sized accounting firm on the outskirts of Detroit. Daniel was still working for an ice cream novelties company, though they had just given him a demotion to an office "out in the boonies," as he referred to it, an hour's drive from the city. And Daniel had always been a city boy—his territory, the small, family-run convenience stores. The company was hoping he'd just pack it in and retire, but for six months he'd been making the long commute each way to sit miserably in a dim, stuffy office, making phone calls and filling out forms. He kept telling everyone at the resort that he was still a salesman, and Maura didn't contradict him. They'd had a brutal winter. She'd let him be a salesman again for a couple of weeks.

"Didn't Groucho Marx sing some song about geraniums?" he asked.

"Groucho didn't sing. He was a comedian," she said.

"Sure he did. He had some hit song about geraniums," Daniel insisted. Most salesmen were Danny, but he was Daniel, even if it was only ice cream novelties.

They had two more days to go, she thought, and here they were arguing about Groucho Marx. "Go blow your nose again," she told him. "You're the only one I know who can go to Florida and get a bad cold." They were on Sanibel Island, though Daniel kept calling it Saint Bell, like he was translating it from the French.

The resort was set up on the cruise ship principle—mountains of food everywhere, all meals included. Nonstop, organized activities like yoga, volleyball, bingo. You ate your meals with other couples and were expected to mingle. Daniel and Maura were stuck at a table with a woman who made hats out of beer cans and kept trying to sell them. Daniel admired her gall. "A good salesman's got to have gall," he told Maura. She and her husband Jerry—"call me Jer"—were from Iowa. They could put the food away. Daniel admired that too. He admired the worst in people, it seemed to Maura sometimes.

Florida had been hit by a fluke winter storm that had damaged the citrus crop and killed a lot of flowers. Maura liked geraniums. She liked to pull off the dead heads after they'd bloomed. She liked to watch the new flowers appear. Their son Daniel Jr. had taken his own life just a month ago. They had debated about canceling the trip. "He would have wanted you to go," Anne, his widow, had told them, though Maura wasn't sure her son would have had an opinion one way or another. He was their quiet child.

"Karaoke tonight," Daniel said. "You gonna sing one of your moon songs?"

"Karaoke is ridiculous," Maura said. She thought karaoke had cheapened her gift. Every time she sang now, she expected someone to sing next, to compete. Her singing wasn't about that. It wasn't about making a fool of yourself, about getting laughed at. She had always gotten up and sang at family gatherings. It was an expected thing—"When is Aunt Maura going to sing?" Even bored teenagers stopped to listen to her beautiful voice. She had developed an entire set of songs about the moon. Maura loved the moon and sang about it with passion. Nights she sang, Daniel fed off that passion to rouse himself and make love to her.

The last time she'd sung was at the funeral. "Amazing Grace"— not even a moon song. "I once was lost, but now I'm found." Danny. Found in his basement with an electrical cord around his neck. By his daughter. Maura couldn't get over the cruelty and thoughtlessness of her own son. She couldn't accept that behind that quiet man could be someone so selfish.

Daniel leaned toward her and sang "Moon over Miami" in her ear, trying to cheer her up. They weren't talking about Danny. Now that Danny was dead, Daniel had taken to shouting everything he said, but nothing he said acknowledged their dead son. Maura thought he might be going deaf, though he had always been loud, overwhelming Danny into a sullen silence when they were together. Their daughter Sandy was called "Sassy" for good reason—she always gave Daniel a run for his money.

"Your face is red," she said. "You'd better put on some lotion."

"It's windburn," he said. "Maybe I should turn over and get it on my back too, for that all-over windburn."

She wasn't worried about catching his cold.

■　■　■

At dinner that night, Rosie, or "Mrs. Bud," as Daniel called her, was sporting her latest creation. It looked like a clown hat to Maura. Rosie called it her Eiffel Tower. Daniel couldn't stop laughing. Rosie was laughing too. Everyone else in the dining room seemed to be laughing. Sitting next to Rosie, Maura was blushing.

It was Baked Alaska Night, and after dinner, all the lights were dimmed as the waiters brought flaming trays to each table.

"Won't you look at that," Jerry said.

"I don't think we have a choice, Bill," Maura said. Daniel nudged her, "Jerry, it's Jerry." He never forgot a name.

After the lights came back on, they all began eating their desserts in silence. It was like the whole stupid thing had humbled everyone, Maura thought.

Lately, Daniel had been saying they should try going back to church, but they hadn't gone. He'd always liked the ceremony of mass, though he hated the sermons. "They should hire me to write their sermons," he used to say. "Spice things up a little." Maura thought he was more interested in the pitch than in what they were selling.

"I wonder who invented Baked Alaska?" Daniel said. His voice seemed unnaturally loud in the sudden silence. No one answered.

"Did I tell you I once met the man who came up with Eskimo Pie?"

"No—really?" Jerry said, leaning toward him.

"Yep."

Daniel often got nostalgic about Bomb Pops, those fat, red-white-and-blue Popsicles that came out for the Bicentennial. He sold a ton of them. They were awkward—you couldn't really get your mouth around them. Too fat to eat quickly like a regular Popsicle, they melted over your fingers. But he loved them, the mess of them, the colors melting together.

Maura knew he was dying in that office. She had tried to talk him into retiring, but he was afraid. His company didn't have a retirement plan, though Maura herself had a decent pension. That, and social security, gave her a comfortable income apart from anything Daniel made, though he still imagined she needed his support.

"Hey, didn't Groucho Marx have a hit song about geraniums once?" Daniel broke the long silence.

"The only song I remember from Groucho was 'Lydia the Tattooed Lady,'" Rosie said.

"That's it!" Daniel shouted, overjoyed. "See, I told you!" he said to Maura.

"What's that got to do with geraniums?" Maura asked edgily. She stabbed her Baked Alaska with a fork, and the ice cream oozed out onto her plate. Maura didn't know whether to use a fork or spoon.

"What's her problem?" Rosie asked.

"Try your spoon, Maura," Jerry said. "It works real good."

Daniel laughed, and Maura could see the Baked Alaska melting in his mouth. The waiters were hovering. Tomorrow was the last night, Tip Night. They had handed out little cards before dinner recommending how much to tip. Maura took out a pen and began writing in the comment section that she was not an idiot and did not need to be told how much to tip. She handed it to Carl their waiter as he refilled everyone's coffee cups.

"You turn those in tomorrow, Mrs. Walston," Carl said. Maura's hand was extended. Carl wasn't coming near that card.

"But I want you to have it *now*, Carl," she said.

"Let me see that," Daniel said, and took the card from Maura. He glanced at it and shook his head, put it in his pocket. "I'll have some things to add to this, Carl," he said. "We'll turn it in tomorrow." He winked at Carl, and Carl winked back.

■　■　■

After dinner, they went back to their room. It was so tiny, Maura felt like they were in a cabin on a ship. She imagined its tilt and rock. She wanted to walk out on deck, but there was no deck. Only a cold evening wind. They were not headed toward a destination. They were marooned.

"Maura, what's wrong?" Daniel asked, surprising her. He usually did not want to know if anything was wrong.

"Nothing," she said. They didn't know how to have conversations like this.

"Well," he said, sounding immediately relieved, "you seem mad at everybody or something." He sneezed twice, then sighed.

Maura stared at the bright red block numbers on their alarm clock: 8:30. "Why do we need to know what time it is?" she said aloud.

Daniel looked at his watch. "Maybe we need some of those drinks with the umbrellas in them."

"We tried that last night," she said. "I want a martini." She stood abruptly and swung open the door.

"Wait, let me blow my nose," Daniel said. She stood in the hall. She could hear him blowing, honking. He was enjoying himself. He was enjoying blowing his nose. She was angry and a little jealous.

■　■　■

The resort had one main bar at its center, near the pool, with all the rooms fanned around it. The food was free, but you paid for your drinks. Rosie and Jerry didn't drink, or maybe they simply did not want to pay, but they hadn't touched a drop the whole trip.

"Probably some religious thing," Daniel had said, shrugging. "Hey, if they can have a good time without it, more power to 'em." Daniel was always giving out more power, even as his own was dwindling.

Sassy had prodded them into going to a support group meeting for families that had experienced a suicide. Daniel took over the meeting, telling jokes, getting everybody to laugh. The group leader got frustrated, but he couldn't complain—wasn't humor one way to cope? In the bathroom, a woman had said to Maura, "He's amazing. You'd never know your son had committed suicide."

Going to the bar was a relief—they could sit wherever they wanted. Maura picked the table furthest from the karaoke set-up. "Hey, there's the Bud Lady," Daniel said. She was sitting up front, wearing a Pabst Blue Ribbon sombrero.

"Sit down, Daniel, before they see us. I'm tired of them."

"Maura, sometimes you're a snob, you know that?"

When her martini arrived, Maura took a long swallow.

"Do you miss Danny?" she asked suddenly.

"Of course I do," Daniel answered. After a long silence, he continued, "but what are we gonna do, be sad the rest of our lives? Of course I miss him. Danny was Danny," he said. "The Scat Man."

"What?"

"Nothing," he said. Wet salt from his margarita clung to his mustache.

"Scat Man? Is that what you called our son?"

"Just a nickname," Daniel said. "You know how he always ducked out of things without saying good-bye. He'd just disappear, and he was so damn quiet you didn't even know he'd left."

"Scat Man," she said softly, "he might have liked that." Her somber son who wrote poetry but showed it to no one. Who collected toy soldiers and set them up at a big table in his basement that his own children could not touch. Who created birthday cards on his computer, but instead of personalizing them tried to make them as close to a store-bought card as possible.

She surveyed the crowd anxiously. She knew it was a matter of time before the hat lady and Jer joined them. What bothered her the most about those two was how they tried to impose their happiness on everyone. Maura wasn't sure she wanted to be happy, not really, not ever again. She played with her stirrer. She wanted to press Daniel about their son tonight, to make contact, to hook somebody else up to her space walk. She wasn't sure that she wouldn't float away pretty soon. She heard a screech in the microphone and looked up.

"Hello, everyone! You like my hat? I made it myself—if you'd like one, I'm sitting over here." Rosie pointed to Jerry, and he waved and grinned. "Anyway, I'd like to sing a song for my new friend, Danny, the ice cream salesman." Maura was afraid to look up. She knew he'd be beaming. "We were talking at dinner about this song, so I'd like to sing it for Danny to show him he was right."

Maura's martini looked like a pool shallow enough to dive in and break her neck. She knew he would let Rosie call him Danny, though he liked to be known as Daniel—Daniel in the lion's den.

The thing was—and everybody seemed to be whispering it to

each other—she sounded just like Groucho Marx. There wasn't really anything about geraniums in the song, but she worked them in, and Daniel poked Maura in the ribs when she did. It was like they were kids playing a foolish game, and Maura didn't have enough imagination to play along. Like her quiet son, who'd sat off to the side reading a book, even when the house was filled with other children.

"She's a dead ringer for Groucho," Daniel said. "I wonder if she can do anybody else?"

"I think just Groucho," Maura said. Around them, people were raising their eyebrows and smoking pretend cigars. The whole world was going insane.

The last time she saw Danny, he came over to return some books he had borrowed. Maura had become an avid reader in her retirement, like she'd always said she would. She never surprised anyone, even herself.

Danny had been a big man, just a bit overweight. He looked like someone who had played football in high school, but he had not. He looked more lively and active than he ever really was. As a child, he'd get picked first in games, and then disappoint who-ever'd picked him.

"Mom," he said, "I didn't have time to read these. I'm sorry," he said. "I didn't want to keep them any longer. They've been sitting on my nightstand mocking me for too long."

"Oh, that's okay," she said. "When you retire, you can catch up," she said.

They both laughed. Danny was a history teacher at the same high school he had attended. Neither of their children had gone far from home, and Maura took it as a compliment that they wanted to stay close, physically close, though with Danny, it was probably because it was the easiest thing to do. He took the least stressful path whenever he could. "It's not worth the trouble," he always said, until no one argued that it was worth the trouble anymore. They just nodded and said, "That's Danny."

He loved his children and his wife, that's what Maura could not understand. How could he leave them like that, the children so young and needy? How could anyone ever get over that kind of abandonment? She knew she couldn't. Wouldn't.

Daniel said he was keeping his job to help Danny's kids, though it turned out Danny had saved quite a bit. He had worked in the summers painting houses with one of his few friends, Lenny, a neighbor boy who never married and still lived with his widowed mother. Lenny always kidded him about how slow he painted, but Danny liked not being controlled by bells, and he worked at his own pace.

When Danny left that last day, he gave no sign, even in retrospect, that he was saying good-bye. Unlike Sassy, he said "I love you" to Maura without being prompted, and he had said it, and he had kissed her cheek and hugged her and driven away like it was an ordinary Saturday in September. The next day he was dead. The books weren't mocking him anymore. Maura had desperately shaken those books to see if Danny had left a note, but there was nothing. They crashed to the floor around her while Daniel tried to hold her still. He didn't cry, but sweat poured down his bald head, glistening in the dim light of their bedroom.

It was getting late, and the karaoke singers were drunk and drunker. Daniel had gone over to the Iowans' table to thank Rosie for the song. Maura had stayed put. When he came back, he said, "She's a genius, that lady. Old Jer's up there taking orders for those hats—they're lining up for them."

Maura had wanted to get drunk enough to sing a moon song, to show Daniel and everyone that she was a person with talent, someone who could do something, who could loosen up, have a good time, but now she couldn't. Rosie had ruined everything with

her performance. It would be a competition now. She excused herself and headed for the bathroom, but instead she felt pulled toward
the path back to their tiny room. She stopped and stood under a
palm tree, took a deep breath. The wind was cool and rattled the
palm fronds so they sounded artificial and plastic.

Daniel had walked up front and grabbed the microphone. She
heard him singing "Danny Boy." She felt like she was on a plunging
elevator—her feet nearly gave way beneath her. Then, she was
rushing forward. His maudlin display was shaming her to tears,
though the crowd was loving it, some of them singing along. No one
knew about their son. It was just a hokey Irish song they all knew
the words to. Daniel was being the fool again. He saw her coming
and held his hand out. His eyes locked on hers. His voice was loud
and clear, and not as bad as Maura always said it was. Maura
stopped near the front row of tables. She had stage fright now, or
something like it. She stood still as he finished, her body trembling.

"And now," he said, "my lovely wife would like to sing a little
song about the moon."

"What moon?" Jerry shouted.

Maura shook her head and started backing away. The levels of
shame were piling up, and the one on top, weighing them all down,
was that she had a son who had taken his own life. She turned and
began running.

Daniel caught up with her as she again reached the lit path to
their room. "Honey, I was trying to close the door on this thing," he
said. He was breathing heavily through his mouth, catching his
breath. "I thought if we both sang a song for him, it'd be like saying good-bye."

"You didn't let me in on your little plan," she cried.

"No. No, I didn't," he said. They were at their door now. Maura
waited for Daniel to fish out the key from his pocket, the big red
plastic "8" clacking against his loose change.

"We have to live with this," she said. "Not say good-bye to it."

"You think more about him dead than you did when he was alive," he said.

Maura stood in the doorway and waited as Daniel flicked on the lights. What he said was true.

"Don't you?" she asked.

"Yeah," he answered slowly. "I guess I do. I keep asking myself, 'what was he thinking?' You were closer to him. He was always a mystery to me."

"Scat Man," she said.

"Yes," he said. He fell face first onto their bed, and for a moment, Maura thought he had passed out, or was having a heart attack, but he then rolled over and groaned, looking up at her. He raised his arms toward her, and she moved toward the edge of the bed and fell into them.

They lay together in silence. "I ordered you one of those hats," he said finally.

"No you didn't," she said, trying not to smile.

"Oh yes I did," he said. She knew her husband. She knew he had. He was already shaping stories from this trip to tell. To who? His old customers? He still wanted to sell something to someone, she could tell. He wanted to be convincing, funny, honest. Someone you smiled at when you saw him walking toward you. Someone whose son would be alive and caring for his young children.

Maura wrapped her arms around his bald head. She cradled it against her chest. "I see the moon, the moon sees me," she sang softly. She trailed off and gently stroked his head.

"Rub it and make a wish," he said. He kissed her through the thin fabric of her dress. She laughed softly. She noticed the door still open behind them, the light drifting into their dark room. She stroked and rubbed, but she could not wish.

Renegade

When I got out of the army, I moved right back in with my parents in Detroit. It was the only place I'd ever lived till I got drafted. Right away, I noticed the rooms seemed smaller. I used to jump up and touch the ceiling, proud that I could reach that high. Some of my old smudges were still up there. All I had to do now was stand on my toes. One of the first things I did was wash those ceilings.

I was used to the lack of privacy, but suddenly it bothered me because it was *my family* I kept running into—in the bathroom, on the stairs—not a bunch of grunts. My parents, my younger brothers, and my sister—they drove me a little nuts. I got a small black-and-white TV and put it in the room in the basement my father had fixed up for me while I was gone. It was nice I didn't have to share a room, but I felt even more separate from the rest of the family down there. Every so often, I'd punch a hole in the cheap plywood. It didn't take much to piss me off back then.

I got a job as quick as I could, and it didn't take long. The car factories were still hiring pretty steady, and my father got my application moved up the list through a guy he knew in the employment office. Some other vets were working in the plant, and we hung together, drinking after work at the Tel-Star across the street. A bunch of them rode bikes and belonged to the Renegades, so I bought a Harley and signed up.

I'd kept my old Plymouth Satellite. Put it up on blocks in the street before I got sent over. When I came back, it was still there, rusting away. I didn't want to claim it. I had a junkyard come haul it away. The bike took up less room. I liked the air slapping at me, even in winter. I enjoyed ripping the ice out of my beard when I got to work. I liked anything that woke me up, even for a second.

The Renegades were pretty pitiful, actually. Our clubhouse, a dark, damp concrete block building, reminded me of the basement I lived in. It was down in the old warehouse district by the Detroit River, and nobody messed with us there. Our neighbors were rats and bums—we fit right in. We played cards, drank, and got high. It was the kind of half-fun I used to have when I'd get a weekend pass. Some of the guys had girlfriends. Most of them were overweight too. We were just a bunch of big fat hogs riding our big fat hogs. On weekends when we weren't working, we went for long rides and terrorized small tourist towns up in the Thumb.

I wasn't one of the guys who was hooked up with an "old lady," as we called them. Hanging around the clubhouse wasn't getting me anywhere either. Though there was some sharing going on, I'd lost my taste for that overseas. Being in the Renegades made me more aggressive when it came to women. It was kind of like, grab them and see what happens.

One night, we were hanging around the clubhouse, as usual. It was mid-June, one of those first really muggy nights, and we had the door open, a bulletproof steel door we all chipped in to buy. Flies and the first mosquitoes were pouring in. Big Bear was cursing. There was a lot of him to bite, and he was being taken advantage of. Bear was one of the few Renegades who wasn't a vet. He was deaf in one ear or something, though he always seemed to hear when he wanted to.

The plant had been brutal that afternoon, so hot everybody just walked off the job in the middle of the shift. Around ten o'clock that night, we were drunk already, swigging them down. Not just because we were thirsty, but because the heat pumped us up, sizzled our little brains, made the clubhouse seem even tinier.

"Let's get the fuck out of here," Bear said. A ride would feel good, I thought. Anything besides another game of pool, a game I never liked much. A group of us hopped on our bikes and hit the road. I took the lead and headed back to my part of town. It was high school graduation time, and I had a feeling we might stumble onto a party or something.

Sure enough, over on Bart, we got backed up in traffic near the Dairy Queen. A bunch of kids were spilling over someone's front yard and into the street. I stopped and turned back to the other guys. "Let's park 'em and look around," I said. "Check out some sweet young things."

Bear laughed and nodded, and we all rode our bikes up onto the sidewalk. It was clear we'd gotten the party's attention. Everyone retreated back into the yard, huddling together in little groups. We took our time parking the bikes, then stepped off and moved toward the party. As soon as I got off the bike, I felt the heat again. We had our colors on, and heavy black boots.

I'm sure some of those kids were pissing their pants, and I took some pleasure in throwing that kind of fear into them, some young punks who wouldn't have to get yanked out of there to fight no goddamn war.

A few jock types huddled up and blocked our way as we pushed toward the keg. Everything got real quiet. Those kids looked so scared, we all just started laughing. I mean, they looked so scared, it made me want to kick their asses even more. I didn't feel any fear, not even a shred of it, and that was disappointing. I kept looking for something to fill this big hole inside me, and fear was one of the few things that took up space in there.

One of the jocks stepped forward. "You guys, you guys weren't invited. We don't know you guys," he said, looking around nervously. "This ain't no open party."

Bear took his time. He was good at this kind of shit. He looked around. "Looks pretty open to me. Now if you excuse me, *punk,* I think I'll grab a brew."

He shoved the kid aside. The kid shoved back. Bear turned around and looked at us. Then he coldcocked the kid, and all hell broke loose. Most of the kids ran, and those that didn't got their asses beat by the Renegades. I was busy punching out one little skinny geek when I felt someone tug on my arm. I grabbed with my free hand—I almost decked him before I realized it was my little brother Teddy. I let go of the kid beneath me. His face was bloody, and he was crying.

I never thought Teddy might be there, though I suppose I should have. Teddy seemed like a straight-arrow wimp. He was on student council and in the National Honor Society. I was six years older than he was, and we never did much together. He used to go to the library with my mother while the rest of us were in the street playing ball. I was a "C" student in high school and took mostly industrial ed. courses. My father didn't know what to make of Teddy either—I think he was hoping for some middle ground for the both of us, the middle ground he'd found as a pipe fitter in the plant, a step above the grunts on the line.

Around the house, he was either staring at my tattoos or ignoring me. It seemed like he studied a lot. We didn't keep the same hours, and I was rarely home much anyway. I even kept some clothes at the clubhouse for those nights when I'd sleep off a hangover on one of the ratty couches.

"What are you doing here?" I said to him. "Get outta here before you get your ass kicked!"

"Take your friends and leave. Please," he said. I was surprised at his calm voice. Looked like it was over anyway—everyone was either scattered, or down.

It was like he'd woken me up from a dream I couldn't quite remember, a bad dream. We looked at each other for a long second. He might have been drunk too—I couldn't tell. I went over and grabbed the keg and hoisted it on my shoulder. "You're too young to be drinking," I said, and tried to laugh. Sirens were approaching. The others were getting back on their bikes. I sent the keg rolling down the street, and we rode off, splitting up quickly. We knew better than to go back to the clubhouse. The cops were sure to show up there.

"Home early tonight," my mother said. "Yeah," I mumbled, and slouched down on the couch to watch Johnny Carson with her. I noticed some blood on my hand, and my stomach knotted up. Ed McMahon was laughing that goofy laugh of his. Ed was a combat vet—he could laugh however he wanted to. I got up and scrubbed my hands in the bathroom. I stood at the sink and let the water run for a long time. When I went to bed, Teddy still wasn't home. In the morning, we sat together for a late breakfast, but neither of us said a thing.

Between work and the Renegades, I didn't stop to think about much. Life went on. I fit right in at the factory with its noise and filth and heat, its booby traps, its guerrillas. The whole place reminded me of the jungle, though on less dramatic terms. The boredom of the job was a relief.

Truth is, I was never the bully type. Never had the size or stomach for it. I've always been on the thin side, except for a little beer belly. In high school, I made my rep by *losing* a fight. This guy was kicking my ass in the Top Hat parking lot, and I kept coming back for more, hanging in there even when I was a bloody mess. It showed everybody I was crazy, taking a beating like that. If you're nuts, they leave you alone. It worked in the army, too.

I don't understand some of the shit I did back in the Renegade days. It was a kind of purge, I guess, for most of us, though guys like Bear were just plain mean, war or no war. I can't forget that party. Someone from my family saw me being an animal. Before, they'd seen the colors, the bike, my rowdy friends who stopped by the house. But without any real evidence, they could imagine I was still a decent person. Teddy sells real estate now. He's the one kid in our family who's made good. Teddy, I'm sorry for what I did.

I didn't go back to the clubhouse that weekend. I rode my bike alone out to Stony Creek where I lay my pale body out in the hot sun until it turned to flames.

■   ■   ■

I married the first woman who didn't run when I grabbed her, then I quit the Renegades. Had to invite them all to the wedding, and they trashed the hall. I think some of those guys would've come after me if they weren't invited. That's the kind of friends I had then, guys so pissed off at the world, you couldn't turn your back on them. I can't believe I rode with them for five years. I think we were trying to make up for the years we lost and just ended up losing some more.

I got most of the meanness out of me now. I'm married again, third time. Marlene, a girl I met through AA. I'm not big on all that touchy-feely, higher-power shit, but man, I needed something. My dad died a few years back. While he was lying there dying of lung cancer, puffing on a cigarette, he told me to get my shit together. I said, "Look at you, smoking a death stick and telling me to get my shit together."

"Yeah, that's right," he said, "look at me. Listen, Kenny, I *know* what I'm doing. Do you know what *you're* doing?" He was taking these long, hard breaths between each sentence. Gave time for it to sink in. I had no fucking idea what I was doing. If he was killing himself and knew it and maybe wanted it, that was his right. If I learned one thing in Vietnam, it was that I did not want to die. Not then, not now.

Well, okay, I am drinking again now, and so is Marlene, but just a couple beers at home. We don't go out anymore. *No more bars,* that's what I finally ended up pledging. They bring out the meanness in me. I was dry for nine months, then one night Marlene and I were sitting around our apartment, watching some goofy talk show, and she asked me about the war.

What I said was, "Bet you five bucks I can sit here and drink one beer, then stop." By the end of the night, it got pretty confusing as to who owed who what.

I've got a decent job now. A cook in a restaurant, if you can believe that. It's no fancy place or nothing. I handle all the grill work. I still keep in touch with my first wife, Jean. We had a kid together—a boy, Jerry. He's fifteen now. Getting into trouble, I'm afraid. I only have him every other weekend, and he don't even want to see me that much. My second wife—well, we were both drunk the whole time. It didn't last long. I could probably get it annulled if I had the energy. I loved Jean, but I was just too messed up in the head.

One night when I was still in the Renegades, I stole a fire extinguisher from a bowling alley and threw it in the back of my dad's pick-up truck that he let me use sometimes. I forgot about it till months later when I see this car in flames. I pull over, whip out my extinguisher, and put out the fire. A cop pulls up. The guy whose car was burning up is all grateful, calling me a hero and stuff, but the cop, he's looking at the fire extinguisher. "Where'd you get that?" he asks.

I tell him I found it in a field, but he takes it, checks the serial number, finds it's stolen, and I'm busted. Can you believe it? From hero to criminal just like that. Kind of like how I felt when I got back from the war. Almost had to serve some time for that fire extinguisher, but I got probation, seeing as I was a vet and all.

We didn't pay no attention to the war. It kind of snuck up on us after high school. Everybody I know who got drafted went. It caught me by surprise how much the war divided everybody up. I missed the sense of togetherness I heard about—"the sixties" and all that. I missed the sex stuff too. I heard over in Nam that everybody back home was fucking like bunnies. Sexual revolution. Shit, I got home and didn't know what the hell to say to a girl. Then I joined the fucking Renegades, thinking I'd get some of that sense of togetherness. I know that sounds crazy, joining a motorcycle gang as a substitute for missing the hippie thing. Marlene tells me there's a pothole in my brain and I keep falling into it. She got me a baseball cap that says "Smoothe Sailing"—I don't know what that "e" is doing at the end of smooth, but I think my life story is the story of that "e."

■　■　■

When I was sixteen and my girlfriend Cheryl was fifteen, we ran away to my uncle's hunting cabin up north near Grayling. Early March. Cold. We huddled together on an old, sagging mattress. I was keeping the wood-burning stove stoked as best I could, but I'd never paid much attention when we were hunting. Fires were my dad's thing, and he always took care of them. Got mad if you messed with his fire.

"What are we gonna do, Kenny?" Cheryl asked.

She was holding her hands between her knees to keep them warm. I had a sore neck from sleeping funny. I rubbed it and rubbed it, pounded at it with my fist. No running water. Only an outhouse in the woods. I hadn't thought of all that when we took off three days earlier after her dad told me to stop coming around.

"Maybe we could drive to Las Vegas and get married," I said. "Then your parents would just have to deal with it."

"Yeah," she said. "It's warm in Las Vegas too."

"I need a fucking shower," I said. I had a hundred and fifty bucks to my name. I tried to calculate if that could get us to Vegas.

"I got some savings bonds from my communion and shit," she said.

"Aw, don't worry about it, Cheryl," I said, though we were both worried. I was halfway through my senior year and hadn't, until we ran off, thought much about what I'd do after graduation. Figured I'd get drafted or get a job in the plant with my dad.

I pumped gas after school and weekends, so I had a little money. I had a girlfriend, my Plymouth Satellite, and a store I could buy beer at. In our neighborhood, the thinking didn't go much beyond that, at least with my friends.

The hunting cabin was actually a lot like the Renegades' clubhouse, except even smaller. Same cinder blocks, same damp, cold air. We used to have farting contests during deer season, the one room packed with all my male relatives. Grandpa came every year till he died, even when he could barely walk.

"Do you love me?" she asked.

"Yes, I do love you, Cheryl," I said, and I looked her in the eye. I tried to light a cigarette, but the matches were wet. When we first got there, we had our first real sex, I mean, total sex. I used a rubber, but I only had one, so after that we went back to groping.

I'm amazed I was sensible enough then to think about the risk of getting her pregnant. Shit, the older I got, the stupider I got, I guess, because that's why I married Jeannie five years later—she was pregnant. The war made me more reckless. Or, more stupid, though some guys would be pissed off at me for saying that.

"Does this mean we're dropping out of school? That's probably not very smart." Cheryl had plans for college. I admired her for that, but those plans didn't rub off on me any.

"Yeah, but your goddamn parents. What can we do about them? I mean, think about it. We go home now, you think there's any chance in hell they're gonna let us go out?"

It had come down to saving face, and we both finally admitted it. We wouldn't be going to Las Vegas. I heated up some baked beans and boiled hot dogs for dinner. We didn't have ketchup or mustard, so we put beans in the buns for flavor.

We went to bed early that night and curled tight around each other in silence. With the cold, and the dark, there wasn't much else to do. We were tired of thinking. We didn't even kiss. Just went right to sleep.

Early the next day, we heard a knock at the door. It was my father. I nodded, let him in.

"Time to come home, Kenny." Then he turned to Cheryl. "Your parents are worried sick about you."

She burst into tears. I looked down at my hands. We packed up what there was to pack, which wasn't much.

"Kenny, that's a shitty fire you've got going there," my father said.

We piled into my car and headed down I-75 back to Detroit. My father followed us to make sure we didn't try to sneak away, though we didn't even think about it. She sat next to me and cried nearly the whole way.

We didn't have much fight left, once we were back home. I couldn't see her, except at school, so we slowly fizzled out. Our circles barely intersected, so it was easy enough to drift apart. Too easy, almost. Cheryl was a sweet girl, and I'll always love her. She shed way too many tears over the whole thing, and I think it finally just wore her out.

Busting up that party. Running away with Cheryl. When I lie in bed at night and start drifting, it's not the war that comes splashing over the side of my leaky boat. It's those two stories.

"You can't pick your dreams, that's what makes 'em weird," my father told me one night after I woke up crying. That's maybe my earliest memory, him hanging over me with his cigarette breath and telling me about dreams and weirdness.

I can't change the stories, but I did change their order. I want to leave you thinking about me and Cheryl driving off into the night, laughing and shaking with what we'd done. I had my arm around her. She was kissing the side of my face. "We're doing it, we're really doing it," she kept shouting. In the rearview mirror, there was only darkness as we headed north. The heater vent didn't work on that old car, so I had wedged a piece of wood in there to keep it open. Wide open heat blowing up at us.

That was the only time in my life I ever really surprised anyone. After that, I sort of fell into line—a squiggly line, but a line all the same. I guess that's kind of ironic, me being a Renegade and all.

Good Neighbor

Bert, our old next-door neighbor, showed up at the front door on one of those gray days in February so dark the streetlights never go off. He lived next door to us for forty years and never did that before— just walked up and knocked on the door.

"Hey, Bert," I said. "Long time no see." He'd moved out of Warren two years ago. I admit, I wasn't unhappy to see him. He reminded me of simpler times in the neighborhood. He gave me a great big hug. I've got a bad back. Spine all twisted up, and there's nothing they can do for me. So it hurt, that hug. I caught my breath and looked up at him. He had this anxious look on his face. I thought he was here to tell me somebody died.

"I was just driving around and thought I'd stop in and see some old neighbors," he said, like we were something to look at in a museum or a cage. I stepped back to let him into our living room. I was wearing an old sweat suit that was all fuzzed up and ratty. It's what I wear most days. Bert had a suit and tie on like he was going to work or something, though he'd retired long ago.

"Have a seat," I said, and punched the remote to turn off the TV. I don't watch much, but I have one story that I follow, and it had just started. The older I get, the crankier I get about missing my story. I'd have to call my sister-in-law Luanne later to find out what happened. Problem with calling Lulu is she always has plenty of real stories to tell, and I'm not so interested in those.

"I'll go get Terry," I said as Bert settled into Terry's brown recliner. I hurried out of the room and found Terry asleep again. "Wake up, wake up," I said. "Bert Crowley's here." Terry, my husband, retired from Chrysler's eleven years ago. He's taken up the computer and loves to say he's "surfing the web," though half the time I go in his little "office"—the boys' old room—he's either playing solitaire or he's asleep in the chair. He says they make chairs too comfortable these days.

He shook his head. "Bert's here?"

I nodded. "He said he's here *visiting*," I said, still puzzled myself.

"I'll be there is a minute," he said. He still had his pajamas on.

"Hurry up," I said, closing the door hard to make sure he was awake.

I went back into the living room. Bert had loosened his tie. "Coffee?" I asked.

"Sure, nothing better than coffee." I could think of plenty of things better. I had some leftover in the pot. I thought about making fresh, but just poured a cup and popped it in the microwave to reheat.

"So, how's Helen and the kids?" I shouted from the kitchen.

"Oh, fine, fine. We just got back from a trip to France with Barb and her husband the lawyer. We stayed at this hotel in Paris you wouldn't believe. Right on the Left Bank," he said. Left Bank, Right Bank, that didn't mean anything to me. I brought his coffee in and put it on a pelican coaster, a souvenir from our trip to Florida.

"Got any milk?" he asked.

Bert had hugged me once before, when he and Helen were having problems. I was a nurse, and the neighbors came to see me for everything, even problems like that. He'd asked me over one afternoon when he should have been at work. I was bringing in groceries when he snuck up on me, whispering that we had to talk. My kids were at school. Helen had taken their kids and left him.

I should have known better to go in that house again. I'd only been there once before, when I'd taken Kelly over to apologize for picking some of Helen's flowers. Kelly was screaming. I was dragging her. She needed to know not to mess with other people's property. Even something pretty like flowers. Looking back, that seems a little harsh. All those firm, clear lines I drew back then seem pretty smudged these days.

Helen held the door open, and I pushed Kelly forward. She had to calm down before she could speak, so we sat in their kitchen waiting for Kelly to catch her breath. Her kitchen had the same clean, sour smell that diners have in the morning when they first open, before anyone's lit up a cigarette or poured a cup of coffee. I didn't get offered any coffee. After Kelly wheezed out her apology, Helen stood. She took the flowers from Kelly's hand and walked to the door. "I was just going out," she said, though she never went anywhere. I took the hint, and we left.

After I put my groceries away, I went over and listened to Bert talk it out. Told him to call Helen at her sister's. My kids would be home from school soon, and I had to get back, I said, and that was true. It was then he hugged me—too tight, pushing himself against my breasts. I had to struggle to get my arms between us and push him away. I hurried home and never told anyone. He was a handsome man and knew what he was doing. I felt like I had the smell of that kitchen on my skin for weeks.

"Sure, sure, we've got milk." I hurried back into the kitchen and brought out some nondairy creamer. Terry's watching his

cholesterol. Now, if Bert wanted to talk cholesterol, we'd have something to talk about, but he was on to his other daughter, Clementine,
who was a nurse married to a doctor. Bert looked strangely at the
carton and shrugged, then drank his coffee black. I looked at my
watch, already tired of Bert taking up space in my house. Why was
he here, I kept wondering, what did he want?

Bert and Helen never fit in with the rest of the neighbors. He
was a salesman down at Jacobson's in Birmingham, where none of
us could afford to shop. They didn't socialize much. We used to talk
over the fence once in a while until the hedge he'd planted grew
too high. Oh, sometimes we'd meet out front and talk, watering the
lawn, stuff like that, but they were never porch sitters like us.

We don't sit out like we used to. Looking across the street at
each other dying off, it's too depressing. What other neighbors was
he thinking about visiting? On the other side of his house lived the
crazy Atwoods. Half of them were in jail, and it was only the mean
old man left there, rotting away behind the peeling paint and weeds.

"You should see the place we live in now—out in West Bloomfield," Bert said. I was thinking, well, invite us then, but he was
pulling out pictures. They'd bought a bigger place, which didn't
make sense to me since it was just him and Helen now. Helen, he
wasn't saying anything about her. I imagined her hiding out in a
dark corner of that huge house. Why they'd stayed married was
anybody's guess.

The house was nice, I suppose. Just a bigger version of what we
have here. His son-in-law the lawyer bought it for him, and there
was a story behind that. I don't think I even heard the boy's name,
so excuse me calling him just "the lawyer." He was representing this
man—an alcoholic, it seems—in a divorce, and the guy had to get
rid of his house right away or lose it to his ex, so the lawyer—*his*
lawyer—made a dirt-cheap offer and bought it for his in-laws.

"Isn't that unethical or something?" I asked.

"Oh, no, no. He just outsmarted the guy. Took advantage of the opportunity. That's how to get ahead in life," Bert said. I was feeling pure pain, as if one more vertebrae in my back was turning to dust as we spoke, my own house crumbling in on me. He didn't seem much ahead of *us* all those years he lived next door. Maybe he didn't get dirty like Terry, but I doubt if he made any more money.

"Len, the young man who bought your house, he's very nice," I said. I didn't know what was taking Terry. "Terry," I shouted toward the back of the house. Len had cut down those big hedges, and we could see in the yard over there for the first time in years.

Len was black. The first black person to buy a house on our block. Though we lived less than a mile from Detroit, our neighborhood had stayed all white for a long time. Some of the other neighbors, if they saw Bert, they'd be giving him a piece of their mind. Us? Well, our son Jim married a black woman, Sonya. It didn't last, but it wasn't her fault. Jim, our Jimmy—nobody could live with him very long—it pains my heart to think of him.

"He still there?" Bert asked.

"You bet," I said. "He's getting married next month."

Bert shook his head. "He gave me more than what I was asking. I had to sell to him." Bert didn't look any happier in his suit and tie than he did puttering in the yard in his Bermuda shorts. What was he trying to prove? Maybe he was driving around looking for a funeral to go to. He was clearly in no hurry to leave. I felt guilty for anything I had ever imagined I might have felt for him all those years ago.

I nodded. Len's a porch sitter. It's nice to have a younger man sitting out there. He works on the house a lot, and he seems full of energy, even when he's just sitting. If somebody wanted to spit on his house or spray it with graffiti, they'd have to do it in front of him, and nobody did. I think Andy Atwood would've if he was younger, but we're not even sure he's alive in there, though a light comes on every night.

Len's a religious sort. Though I've never been a churchgoer, I've started asking somebody to stop this pain in my back. I like to catch Len on a Sunday, when he's all spiffed out. I doubt he goes to a church around here, but he goes somewhere.

I kept waiting for Terry to emerge. I kept waiting for Bert to ask about Terry, our kids. The kids are all a mess, but I could've made up some good stories, and besides, there were all their pictures sitting right on top of the TV, reminding him that we've got a family too.

It was rude of Terry not to join us, and we weren't a rude family. There they were—Jimmy, Eric, Kim, and Kelly. And the grandchildren, Millie and Jack. Five divorces among four kids probably sounds bad. I can't explain it—Terry and I never talked much, so maybe that set a bad example. We never fought though. The one I miss the most is Sue, Eric's ex. She was the first one. I didn't know any better back then and took her into my heart. Fourteen years later when they split up, it was almost like losing a child.

"Excuse me," I said, and got up again. "Terry, he sleeps a lot these days." Terry was ten years older than me, which was starting to seem like a long time. Terry and I have been married forty-seven years. I love the man. He's all I ever knew.

"You mean it was no big deal, me selling to that colored guy?" Bert asked.

I kept walking to get Terry. Is that why he'd come here? Was he suddenly feeling guilty for that? Nothing was a big deal to us anymore. Everybody just lived. Tried to keep on living. The doctors say I'll eventually be confined to a wheelchair, and Terry, he'll be no good pushing, and what was I gonna do then, and did it really matter who lived next door or what kind of car he drove?

Terry wasn't asleep, but he was dressed. He was playing solitaire again. I whispered loud in his ear, "What are you doing? Our old neighbor Bert's here to visit!" I shook him till his eyes focused on mine.

"Is that so?" he said. Though he slept a lot, it wasn't like him to be forgetful like that. It threw a terror into my heart, wondering if that was the beginning of it, the big forgetting.

"Yes," I said, "and he hugged me."

"Hugged you?" he said, raising his voice. We stared at each other for a long while, letting that sink in. I could have left Bert out there forever, but finally Terry got up, and we went into the living room together.

Bonus

It's humiliating, sucking up to relatives for jobs. Not a lot of folks in my family can do much about getting anybody a job, but I've hit them all up: Cousin Larry got me in at the grocery store as a bagger (a pretty good gig till we went out on strike and they fired us all and got away with it), Aunt Fiona let me work at her Dairy Queen one summer and paid me more than she had to, Uncle Stan got me in at the Ford plant (laid off in six months).

My family, it's good family, though alcohol wiped out my dad and two uncles—and one cousin, beautiful Debbie. We know how to throw a good party, even if it kills us, and Cousin Freddy's annual pig roast at his place out in the country was no exception. Some of the young bucks were already drunk and couldn't wait, ripping half-cooked meat off the damn pig.

I wasn't a young buck anymore, and my prospects, as they say, weren't looking up. I was twenty-six and had just moved back into my mother's house. Earlier that afternoon, I'd exchanged punches with my older brother, Timmy, because he said I was hiding under my mom's skirts. We didn't draw blood or nothing. Just like when we were kids.

Last year after our dad died, Timmy had his stomach stapled up, lost all this weight, and got married, so he'd been thinking he's hot shit. Since my dad died, I haven't been able to focus on much of anything. It didn't seem to bother Timmy none, though my mother claimed he kept it all inside. We all knew it was coming— doctor told my dad flat out if he didn't quit drinking, he'd be dead in a year, and he was right. But I've always been good at putting off the truth—trying to cheat another thousand miles out of bald tires, getting a blowout on the freeway.

Fighting with Timmy got me going. I had to get a job soon, or I really would be a momma's boy. Uncle Lester was my last shot. I swallowed the warm backwash of my fourth beer and edged over next to him.

"Uncle Les?"

He was sipping wine. Something he picked up from his new wife. He sighed, "Yes, Bobby."

He was still calling me Bobby. Not a good sign. I've been trying to change to Rob for years.

"Uncle Les, I'm not gonna shit you, I need a job. You got any-thing at the store for me?"

I'd resisted Uncle Les. He owned a large clothing store in West Bloomfield—one of Detroit's snooty suburbs—and I did not want to be trying to sell shit to rich people.

He looked me over and sipped at his wine. "You ready for sales, Bobby? Commission work?"

My stomach growled. I wanted to be over with the young cousins eating raw meat—anything but this.

"Sure am, yes, I really am." I tried my best, but I was staring at the ground when I said it.

"Listen, Bobby." He put his hand on my shoulder. "You couldn't sell *me* a new suit. You're just like your dad." I winced. I never drank more than six beers anymore, and no hard stuff. I was melting into a warm piece of shit beneath his hand.

"Just give me a chance," I said. Damn it, I was almost crying.

He paused and sighed again. "I can get you in the stockroom, but you know it doesn't pay much."

I knew Uncle Les was no Aunt Fiona, and he wouldn't be paying me anything more than a—than a stock *boy*. My unemployment from the factory job had run out months ago. "I'd like that, Uncle Les," I said.

"No experience necessary," he laughed.

"But I have experience," I said.

"I'm sure you do," he laughed again. I looked around at the pig carcass, half-charred, half-raw meat. Cousin Joe was puking off to the side. Uncle Les's new wife, Cindy, came up and grabbed his arm. Uncle Les had been married so many times, we didn't call his wives "aunt" anymore.

"Come by the store on Monday. I just fired this kid last week." *Kid.* I was about to ask him exactly how much it paid, but thought better of it. I didn't even have gas money for my old rust bucket. I swore I wasn't going to live with my mother more than a year. I promised myself the job would just be temporary.

I walked off and stood by myself on a hill on the edge of Freddy's property overlooking his neighbor's Christmas tree farm. Freddy'd done all right. Since he drove trucks cross country, it really didn't matter where the hell he lived, so he bought himself this nice property—out near Brighton, about an hour north of Detroit. He had his own rig and was his own boss, kept his own hours. He'd once been my drug source—truck drivers have access to the best speed. Though I had no desire to do speed anymore—if anything, I wanted to slow things down.

I looked out at all those green trees swaying in the warm wind.

They reminded me of my father dancing at family weddings. He didn't move much. Just this gentle sway, his drunken arms draped over my mother's shoulders, his eyes closed, the wisp of a grin on his lips. I think I loved him the most when I was watching him dance.

■ ■ ■

Uncle Les was true to his word, and by Monday afternoon, I was wearing a name tag which I'd had them type *Rob* on, and I was unloading a UPS truck full of boxes, getting advice from Byron, the other stock boy, on the finer points of dolly maneuvering.

I didn't see much of Uncle Les around the store, and he barely acknowledged my presence when I did bump into him. Some days, I never even saw him. The other employees kidded me as soon as they found out I was Uncle Les's nephew. They started calling me Baby Huey because I was a little chubby. Byron had been working there for six years, but he was still three years younger than me. He was the pet of all the saleswomen. He was going to college at night, and was nearly through with his engineering degree. "Two more semesters," he said, "and I'm out of here."

I looked like a real loser compared to him—and being Uncle Les's nephew to boot. Byron, to give him credit, sat with me at lunch and brought me into the circle, so that after a couple of months, I felt like a part of the Lester's Best family, even if I was Baby Huey.

Byron and I often stayed late to restock the shelves so everything would be ready when the store opened the next morning. The salespeople took off at six o'clock, on the dot. When it got close to Christmas, the store stayed open till nine, and we often worked until eleven restocking. Uncle Les stayed late too. He liked to be the one to lock the doors.

■ ■ ■

I'd had a crush on my beautiful cousin Debbie. My family might seem a little nuts, eating raw meat and all, but we were civilized most of the time, and we didn't go around hitting on our own cousins. I think she liked me too, though, back when we were fourteen, fifteen. I held her hand once behind the garage at Timmy's high school graduation party. She had found me back there chewing on weeds and feeling sorry for myself. I could only handle so much of the family drinking and bullshitting. My father was really tanked that afternoon. And hell, I was a teenager and hated being around my parents anyway.

I half-enjoyed being lonely back there, the voices and laughter quiet in the distance, the setting sun squeezing in between two garages just to find my pimply little face. But when Debbie rounded the corner, my heart did what hearts do when they're surprised by love.

"Hey stranger," she said.

"Hey," I said, smiling and squinting up at her.

"Is this seat taken?" she asked, and sat down in the weeds next to me without waiting for a reply. My father didn't believe in worrying about growing grass where no one could see. He stored rusty junk back there, stuff that didn't fit in the garage—a shovel with a broken handle, the frame for a go-kart, remnants of a couple of lawn mowers.

"Man, your dad's really loaded today," she said, blowing imaginary smoke rings.

"What else is new," I said.

"He's really giving my dad some shit." She emphasized *shit* with an edge that made me feel somehow responsible.

I shook my head. Uncle Les was Debbie's father. Debbie was from his first marriage, to Aunt Tracy. Back then, Tracy was in and out of institutions for schizophrenia, and Uncle Les was busy with Sally, wife number three, so Debbie grew wild, like one of those weeds.

"How's your mom?" I asked.

"Okay," she said without expression. Then, "I guess," which meant "no."

My father, who worked on the line at Union Carbide, gave Uncle Les a hard time for having an easy job, not getting his hands dirty, and he always quizzed Uncle Les on how he was treating his employees, what benefits they got, etc. My dad was only a union man when it suited his own purposes. When it came to Uncle Les, my dad was Mr. Rank-and-File. They were brothers with six years between them. My father was the older one. They'd never been close. With family, I didn't have to apologize for my father. They knew what to expect.

"Listening to any good tunes these days?" I asked. Debbie and I always talked rock 'n' roll. We listened to the same radio stations and exchanged albums to tape. Neither of us was doing well in school, and we shared the bond of failure—though I'd never been held back a year like she had. For a girl to be held back was a scandal, but she seemed oblivious to it, more determined than ever not to succeed.

"Nah. Nothing sounds good lately," she said softly. "Nothing." I nodded silently, then reached out and put my hands on top of hers in the grass between us. She turned her hand palm up and squeezed mine. I admit, while she sat there in her pretty white blouse confessing her sadness, I was studying how the sun shone to reveal her white bra underneath. Her long, dirty-blonde hair hung straight over her shoulders and down her back, and her herbal shampoo cast a spell over me like incense in church.

It felt good to just sit there alone together—the simple comfort of it, her warm moist hand in mine, the drunken party fading behind us. She didn't have to tell me why she was sad. It was how I felt too. It wasn't any one thing. It was everything, the big rainy world out there, and the leaky roofs of our family.

Then Timmy came back, a little drunk himself, because "wasn't he eighteen years old after all, and a high school graduate," my father'd told my mother as he opened beers for himself and Timmy before the party even started.

"So what have we here? Kissing cousins?" Our hands separated instantly, and we looked at each other with a frantic mixture of fear and love. Timmy turned and rushed back to the party. We hurried behind him, but there was nothing we could do. The old brown paint had turned to dust on the back of the garage, and both our backs were stained with it. Debbie slipped out the gate and down the street while I watched Timmy tell our father God knows what. They were across the cracked driveway from me, so I could not hear their voices above the screaming little cousins and the ball game on the radio. Next thing I knew, my father was backhanding me across the face and shoving me into the house, where he could whale on me in private. I fell into tears, face down on my bed. The loud voices of my parents and Uncle Les raged on outside, then I heard cars quickly pulling away. Timmy came in and yelled at me for ruining his party, then he fell on his bed, face down like me, and passed out.

I know Timmy sounds like a shit, but while I was a little chubby, he was enormous and hadn't had a date all through high school, and he was, I think, a little in love with Debbie himself. Maybe he thought acting like my dad was the way to get approval. It took a staple in the stomach and being "born again" for him to get his act together. "Born again"—my mother and I shared a laugh about that. "Who gave birth to him this time?" she wondered.

Debbie OD'd at age twenty in her dorm room at the end of exam week. In the official Uncle Les version, it was an accident, but she knew what she was doing. He'd insisted she go to college. She got in at Central, one of the easier state schools, but she was partying all the time—flunking out, she'd confided to me at Thanksgiving, the last time I saw her.

Since I moved back home, I've started sitting behind the garage again, even though it's just my mother and me now, and I can be alone all I want.

■ ■ ■

My father had a point about how Uncle Les treated his employees. Seems like he fired somebody every so often just for the hell of it. Right before Christmas, he'd fired this poor girl just because she took some gift boxes home to wrap her own presents in. I mean, the boxes were empty.

I kept quiet and kept those shelves stocked. Uncle Les started calling me Rob, and I was grateful for that small gift. The money wasn't much, but since I was living at home and not paying rent, I was actually building up a little savings, though every morning I prayed my car would start, that it would hang on at least one more year. With Byron's encouragement, I'd signed up for a computer science class at the community college. I was enjoying it, working hard. A lot of the students were older, so I didn't feel like a loser. We were all in it together, trying to figure things out a little late, but maybe not too late. I was losing weight, and doing one hundred sit-ups each night before I went to bed. I'd had coffee twice after class with a cute blonde divorcée with two kids who was telling me every little secret of her life. It seemed like she had a lot more to tell, and I was hoping she did. For a few hours every week, I felt like I was doing high school over again, doing it right.

The store was making a ton of money during the Christmas rush, and Uncle Les was in a good mood most of the time. One day when we were tag-teaming a big delivery truck with our two-wheelers, I asked Byron whether there'd be Christmas bonuses.

"Just for the salespeople. Sometimes," Byron said, and winked. "Your uncle likes the cute ones." Then he moved uncomfortably close to me as I bent over a stack of boxes. "Unless you want to take your own bonus," he said. He hesitated, like there was more, but then he walked away, wheeling a high load of boxes out of the truck so I could not see his face.

Another night when we were working late, restocking, I grabbed him over by Men's Shirts. "Byron," I said, "how do you take your own bonus?"

"Hey, you're not narking for your uncle, are you?"

I stood behind a stack of boxes loaded with Arrow shirts in all colors and sizes. I pulled at the collar of my T-shirt. We didn't have to wear ties like the salespeople. Was I? Was I gonna be a narc for Uncle Les? Did it depend on what Byron was going to tell me? Byron had heard me bad-mouth Uncle Les often enough to know I had no great love for him. Maybe I'd laid it on a little thick just to get accepted. I already felt like I was betraying family, but I hadn't done anything except complain.

I sighed deeply. He didn't seem worried. "Hey, I'm out of here in a few months anyway," he said. "This is my last Christmas. I'm trying to show you something, do you a favor. Help you get out and get your own place." Byron was living at home too, but the whole college thing put a different spin on it. And he was younger. "It's for a good cause. I call it the Byron Murphy College Fund," he laughed.

When we'd work late, Byron would slip some things out on the loading dock, then hide them behind the dumpster. In the darkness, he could easily retrieve the stuff later.

"Hey, Uncle Les is pretty sharp. How come he hasn't caught you?" I asked. My stomach was sloshing with what Debbie and I used to call "bad karma," though I never exactly knew what karma meant.

"It's simple. He trusts me."

It wasn't that simple. Byron had partners. But the trust, that was a big part of it. After Christmas, when all the returns came in, his friends returned the stuff he'd stolen. We catered to a clientele with bucks, and I guess it was considered unseemly to ask for a receipt if the customer didn't have one. If it was an item the store sold, you could get cash back, no questions asked. Christmas bonus.

Byron either liked me or felt sorry for me, or both. He had an upbeat take on everything. He was going places, and I wanted to follow him, at least part of the way. I'd felt defeated when I'd started there, ripe for being taken in by Byron's charm. Hell, even Uncle Les liked him. Though he was years younger, I tended to look at him like an older brother. Timmy? I couldn't say a word to him about anything. "When are you going to grow up?" Timmy always said. I didn't have an answer for that, and if I did, I wasn't going to give it to my big brother.

I thought our dad's death or Timmy getting his stomach stapled might change something between us, but we still ended up at each other's throats at every family gathering. It was like we were locked in stone and could only crash into each other and bounce off.

"It's only a few hundred a year," Byron said.

"Hey, that's probably more than any bonus Uncle Les gives out."

"Well, there you go," was all he said to that, and shrugged.

But still, it was *Uncle* Les. I wished immediately that Byron hadn't told me, though I couldn't blame him. I was the one who'd brought it up again. Just then, Uncle Les came by, banging a clipboard against his thigh.

"You guys almost ready to go? Ten minutes," he said, moving quickly past us.

"We gotta hustle these shirts," Byron said, and that's what we did.

Once Byron told me what he was doing, I tried to avoid him after the store closed. I didn't want to witness anything. Byron seemed sure I wouldn't tell, even though I'd told him I didn't want any part of the action myself. Part of me wanted in, and part of me wanted to tell Uncle Les.

■ ■ ■

After Debbie died, Uncle Les gave me all of her record albums. They were sitting on the porch one day when I got home from work. I brought them in, took them to my room, and stacked them alphabetically, mixing them with my own. I even saved the doubles, twinning them.

I don't remember much of what Debbie and I said to each other back when we were favorite cousins. It's like those records. I can't remember why we liked a lot of them—I stare at the album covers and shake my head. I don't even have a turntable that works. I listen to tapes or CDs, if anything. The records anchor one corner of my room, their frayed, dusty covers holding each other up.

The week before Christmas. December 21, the date Debbie died. I'd never seen Uncle Les on the anniversary, and I was curious to see how it affected him. After closing time, I went back to his office, where he was shuffling stacks of inventory reports.

He looked up. "Rob. What's up?"

"Hi, Uncle Les," I started. I wasn't ready to talk, but he was waiting. I tried to study him for traces of grief.

"Uncle Les, do you give out Christmas bonuses?" I asked.

He laughed. "Not to someone who's only been here a few months. Even if you are family."

"You mean, like, Byron gets one."

"Sure, Byron's proven himself here."

Oh, shit, I thought. Everything was tilting on me. Where was I going now? "You know, today's the day. The day Debbie died."

He quickly turned and lashed out. "Of course I know. What do you expect me to do, close the store? Wear black? I mean . . ."

"I still miss her," I interrupted. In our family, you didn't talk about dying or loving. You grabbed another beer, you playfully punched each other in the gut and said, "You're not getting serious on me, are you?" No wonder Timmy bailed out on us and started talking to Jesus.

Uncle Les sighed. "Listen. Do you doubt that I do? Every year, I try to keep as busy as I can just to get through the fucking day," he said, his voice rising again. He looked tired. "Is that all you came to say, 'can you give me more money and don't you miss your dead daughter?'"

"I was never good with words, you know that. That's why you made me a stock boy," I said, trying to smile, though tears were finding their crooked way down my cheeks.

Uncle Les smiled tightly. He stood up, came around the desk, and put his arm around me. "We can't have our friend Byron walking by and seeing us bawling like a couple of . . ."

He didn't finish, and I couldn't finish for him. A couple of what? And what about Byron, who had lied to me, who now had made it easy for me to betray him? I said nothing. I did nothing. It was the kind of compromise I knew I would have to make to get on with my life.

His arm fell off my shoulder as he led me back into the store. Our little moment was over. I was a stock boy.

"Do you ever listen to those records?" he asked, stopping in the aisle. "Her records?"

I turned back toward him. "No," I said, though I sometimes fingered the album covers and traced the letters where she'd scrawled her name.

It doesn't matter if I took anything or not, and I might have taken a few things after all. It doesn't matter if I happened to have given her the drugs she took to kill herself, and maybe I did. What matters is that I went home and tossed those records. It cleared out a lot of room. Kind of like getting your stomach stapled shut and watching the weight disappear. What I was going to do with that room, I had no idea.

Fireworks

"Congratulations on your promotion," Ken said, shaking my hand after Ellen and I had pulled in, leveled off our camper, and popped open our first beers. I'd bought one of those pop-up tent campers a couple of years back because I was getting too old to sleep on the cold ground, but I'd been so busy at work, we'd barely used it.

Ken and Louise had arrived hours before us, having gotten an early start to avoid the Fourth of July traffic coming over the Ambassador Bridge from Detroit. We were camping together at the Pinery over on the Canadian side of Lake Huron.

"Some fucking promotion," I said. It was my first weekend off in two months. My beer was oozing foam. I kept slurping till it finally stopped.

"Got a live one there, eh Lar?"

"Yeah, but I got it under control now." I smiled and wiped the foam off my upper lip. The kids were already off somewhere.

"Last two guys took that job had heart attacks," I said.

"No shit," Ken said. "Sounds like your job's more dangerous than mine."

Ken was a cop. Not too bright, but sincere. We coached the boys' basketball team together in the winter. Because of work, I often missed practices, but I helped out when I could. He was a good coach—fair—and the kids were drawn to him. He was a leader in a way I'd never be. That was the problem with my new job. I had to be a boss—crack the whip, kick ass. I was used to being one of the guys, making smart remarks and teasing the boss's secretary. But when Lovelock keeled over right in the office, I was next in line.

I'd been an accountant in the controller's office at the Chrysler plant since I got out of the army twelve years earlier. I was supposed to try and make the numbers work while the guys out in the plant were counting rejected parts, breaking the counters on their machines, the night shift stealing from the day shift, double-counting the same parts, ghost employees, guys who on paper worked ninety-six hours straight. It was all supposed to make sense, right? The guys in the plant hated me. I could feel it when I walked down the wide aisles past their machines in my jacket and tie and shiny, steel-toed dress shoes, sparkling safety glasses, and regulation earplugs. Most of them didn't wear earplugs or safety glasses—they didn't care if they went deaf and blind. They hated their jobs worse than I hated mine.

■　■　■

Later, when we heard yelling and screaming from across the campground, Louise and I ran over to where the boys were gathered around a garbage can. They were kicking the can and shouting like a lynch mob.

"What the hell are you kids doing?" I spit out my cigarette and stomped on it, but the ashes kept smoldering in the loose gravel.

"We caught a coon," Toby, my oldest, said.

"Yeah," Jimmy said, "and we're gonna kill it." Jimmy was ten—

Toby's age. Mike, Jimmy's brother, was six, and my other son, Brad, was eight.

"Nobody's going to kill anything," Louise said. "Kids, get back. Uncle Larry's going to let it go." Their kids called me and my wife Uncle Larry and Aunt Ellen, though our kids didn't call Louise and Ken aunt and uncle.

I looked at Louise and laughed. "Oh yeah? . . . Okay, I guess so." The kids backed up. "Further," I said. I stomped on my cigarette again till it disappeared in gravel, then I cautiously approached the dented, brown can. I'm a city boy. We'd started camping because it was all we could afford to do, not because of any great love of nature. I wished Ken was there. He'd taken Ellen out to pick up hot dogs and marshmallows for the campfire. The coon was clearly pissed off, banging against the sides. I took a deep breath, reached for the lid, and yanked. Nothing. It wouldn't budge.

"You kids got this lid on nice and tight, didn't you?" I shouted.

Louise was laughing. "Put down your beer and try two hands."

I walked back and handed her the beer. By now, the kids were screaming and jumping up and down, and a crowd of curious campers had gathered in the dusk. I quickly rushed up and yanked the lid off, then backed away. The coon's hiss echoed off the sides of the can, but it couldn't climb out. Another man kicked the can over, and the coon scrambled out and trotted back into the woods, turning to hiss once more, staring at us scornfully through its mask.

"Kind of spooky, huh?" Louise said as we gathered our kids and turned to walk back to our adjacent campsites.

"Yeah," I said. "Where's Ken when you need him?"

"Oh, he would've just shot the damn thing," Louise laughed. "That's his solution for everything."

I laughed too. Louise was a smart-ass like me. Ken loved to hunt, and every year he tried to get me to go. I'd never fired a gun since the army. I liked fishing, dropping my line down into the dark water and seeing what happened, but hunting was another story.

"Larry, are you okay? Your hands are shaking," Louise said, stopping in the middle of the road. She handed back my beer and gently put her other hand in the middle of my back. I tensed up in surprise, though I liked her hand there.

"Yeah," I said. "A little edgy with all the shit at work." Her hand dropped away. She made a humming noise and shook her head, then continued walking.

Louise wore tight jeans and a T-shirt tucked in snug to reveal her shapely figure. She and Ken both looked great. Ellen and I had sort of let things go, putting on pounds in the usual places. I sat at a desk all day and ate lousy cafeteria food. By the time I got home, the kids had usually eaten already, so I'd wolf down heated-up leftovers in the kitchen by myself. Ellen never gave in—dinner was served at 5:30, no matter how late I had to work. She didn't want to accept my being gone as anything but temporary, though the overtime and six- and seven-day weeks had been pretty much the norm for years, with no end in sight.

Ever since the promotion a month earlier, it'd just gotten worse. I wasn't sleeping, even though I was exhausted. My mind was tired, but my body had been asleep at the desk all day. I started drinking myself to sleep, a few beers every night. But then my stomach started acting up. I tried sleeping pills, but they made me groggy in the morning. So there I was, crunching over the rocky dirt road, thinking how nice it'd be to sleep with Louise, though she was Ellen's best friend and I knew she wouldn't have me. I laughed to myself. I didn't have time to have an affair, even if I wanted to.

The sun was falling fast behind the trees. When we returned to our campsites, Ken was building an intricate teepee of sticks with wadded-up newspaper caged at its center, ready to be sacrificed. Ken was one of those guys who prided himself on starting a fire with one match. Me, I'd drench the wood in charcoal lighter and throw on a box of matches—it drove him crazy. Ken wouldn't let me do the fires anymore.

"You're in charge of cold beer, Larry, and I'm in charge of fires," he'd say. I always kept one cooler stocked. When we were camping, we started in on the beer pretty early, all of us, and kept a semi-steady buzz going until we doused the campfire and went to sleep.

The campground was packed. People at the site behind ours set up a portable TV on their picnic table. It was noisier and less private than at home. Canada celebrated their independence day on July 1, so between the first and the fourth, fireworks were going off everywhere except in our camper.

That night after the fire, Ellen climbed into our double sleeping bag and curled up against me. "Brrr," she said. "It's cooling off out there."

"Clear night," I said. "Lots of stars." She put her cold hands around my belly and slid them down into my shorts.

"Hey," I whispered, "what's the big idea." The kids were asleep behind the curtains, one on the dinette that folded down, and one on the other folded-out wing.

"We can be quiet," she said. That was true. We'd been nothing but quiet lately, exchanging information but little else.

We both missed sex. It had changed after the kids were born, like it does for everybody, I guess. We struggled to get them asleep and still have enough energy left for each other. Then, when overtime started building up, well, our sex life had just about disappeared into a tiny flickering speck in the sky. Ellen, to her credit, was trying to fan that small spark. I turned and kissed her. The people in the silver Airstream trailer on the other side of us were still up, laughing too loud, talking about somebody throwing up in a car.

I came, Ellen didn't. There wasn't much room in that double sleeping bag to be creative. She sighed, "It's okay." I stopped touching her, and she pulled me to her in a long, hard hug. I couldn't even remember how to touch my own wife. Someone walking to the bathroom waved a flashlight in the air, and it passed over our camper in random accusation.

■　■　■

It rained Saturday, so Ken and I drove the boys into Grand Bend, the closest town. In the drizzle, we hit the brewer's retail, the arcade, the souvenir shops, and the fireworks store. One thing I had enough of was money. The overtime pay kept stacking up. I didn't know what to do with it, so I'd started making extra payments on the mortgage.

The boys were old enough to be into fireworks big time. They were motioning to me and holding up a whole brick of Zebra firecrackers. Fireworks had the added attraction of being illegal back in Michigan.

"What are you going to do with a whole brick?" I asked Toby.

"Blow up stuff," he said.

"I want to take it home and show my friends," Brad said.

"Maybe we can sell some," Toby said.

"Hey, I don't want you selling any and having somebody's parents calling me up. We get these, and you've got to use them only when I'm around."

Brad rolled his eyes. "Then we'll never be able to blow up anything."

Ken was picking up some bottle rockets and flares to light off down by the beach. The store was packed with gunpowder. I could smell it—like the whole place was breathing, and one small cough or sneeze could blow us all up. I lay the brick on the counter. "Now, this uses up all your souvenir money," I cautioned.

Ken looked over at us. "You're not gonna bring any of those back over the border, are you?"

"Well, I don't know," I said nervously. "What are you gonna do, bust me, Ken?" I said, trying to laugh.

Ken smiled thinly. "Hey, those border cops don't mess around."

I turned to the counter and paid for the brick. "He's right, you know," the clerk said as he handed me the change.

"Yeah, he's always right," I said, grabbing the brick like a football and charging toward the door.

We drove back to camp, Ken and I sitting silently in the front seat while our boys whispered together behind us. Ellen and Louise were a little drunk. They'd made a crude version of margaritas. A pile of wet salt clung to the picnic table while Louise tried to rim some plastic cups in it.

"Think you guys got enough?" Louise asked, staring at the bags of fireworks.

"Think you girls have had enough?" Ken countered with a smile.

"We're gonna take these home," Toby said, hefting the brick in the air.

"Let me hold it," Brad said, reaching up for it. Toby shoved him away.

Ellen blanched and swallowed the rest of her drink. "You boys give those to your father right now." I took the brick from their upraised hands and held it in mine. I didn't know where to put it, so I went back to the car and threw it in the trunk.

"Dad, aren't we gonna blow any of them off?" asked Brad.

"Later," I hissed.

My boys walked off sullenly. "Anybody need a drink," Louise asked, and I said that I did.

■ ■ ■

Saturday night was strained. Ken conscientiously lit off every single firework he'd purchased. The bottle rockets sparkled above the lake. I didn't even take the brick out of the trunk. My boys half-heartedly waved sparklers. I'd lost count on my beer tally, though Ellen had returned sober from Margaritaville. She seemed half–hung over, so it was hard to read her mood.

After the boys were asleep, we headed off to the bathrooms together. I held my toothbrush tight in my fist. Ellen held the flash-light, though it dangled loosely in her hand, the light swaying any which way.

"Why did you let the boys get all those firecrackers?"

"Hey, they wanted them. I'll supervise, don't worry."

"Ken says you shouldn't take them across the border."

"It's not like we're drug smugglers or something. Ken's got to let his job go. He's like your brother who can't stop selling—shit, Joey can't even get me a beer without trying to sell it to me."

"Oh, look who's talking about not letting his job go," Ellen said. We were standing in a muddy puddle under the yellow floodlight outside the bathrooms.

"Hey, I'd love to let that job go," I said to her. "Fucking love it. Ken should mind his own fucking business." I couldn't remember a time that day when Ken would've had a chance to lecture Ellen on my crimes.

"Quit talking like that. *Fuck* this, *fuck* that. Cussing out your own best friend. Maybe your *only* friend. Listen, I don't want you taking those firecrackers back into the country. There's a reason they're illegal, you know. Larry, Fourth of July's over. I don't want the boys . . ."

Just then Ken and Louise emerged from the darkness. Ken was carrying his monster police flashlight, and I should have seen him coming. He hit me right in the face with that bright white light.

"Okay, hands above your heads," he said. I couldn't see his face. I didn't know how much they'd heard. Out in the woods, sound car-ries for miles.

"What, are you two waiting in line? Must be a good movie," Louise said, smiling tightly.

"You two can go ahead. We're trying to save the world out here," I said, and forced a laugh.

"Or maybe just our marriage," Ellen said under her breath, but loud enough for everyone to hear.

"Give me the fucking toothpaste," I said. She reached into her bag and threw the tube on the ground. I picked it up and stormed into the bathroom, Larry right behind me. He put his big hand around my neck as I stood at the sink gripping the sides with both hands. I tried to take a deep breath. I belched up sour air.

"Hey," he said, either as a warning, or maybe he was simply puzzled.

"We'll be all right," I said, and filled my mouth with toothpaste, scrubbing till foam slid down over my chin.

"Hey," Larry said again, turning his head from above the urinal where he was peeing. "Let's talk. Soon. Really talk."

"Sure, Ken." I said. The women's room was right next door. The walls didn't even go all the way up, but I heard nothing from the other side.

■　■　■

Ken and Louise left early Sunday morning. He was obsessed with avoiding traffic. They had a regular trailer and could just hitch it up to their car and drive away. They only lived five blocks from us back home—though we hadn't seen much of them lately, and after this weekend, we'd see them even less.

"Good-bye Uncle Larry, good-bye Auntie Ellen," their boys called. I wondered when they'd stop calling us that. I'd been spending so little time with my own boys, *they* should've been calling me Uncle Larry.

"We'll see you, boys," I said. Ellen kissed them both. I shook Ken's hand stiffly, and our wives embraced, but we didn't cross over.

I wanted to stay longer. Spend a little more time with my boys.

But nobody could relax, so after lunch we cranked the camper down and took off. Those things are pretty ingenious, when they work right, but ours always seemed to jump the track, get a snag somewhere. That day, we had trouble getting one of the latches hooked, so Ellen and I both had to throw our weight on top of it until it clicked into place.

On the drive home, Ellen wouldn't speak to me. The boys in the back were subdued, staring out their separate windows. We sat in a long line of cars returning to the States after the holiday weekend, inching forward in silence at the border crossing in front of the bridge.

"Are you gonna tell them about the firecrackers?" Brad asked.

"Shhhh! You wanted the damn things, now just sit there and shut up!" I yelled.

Brad started to cry. Ellen turned and smacked me in the face. She had never hit me before. I just stared at her. My lip began to bleed. A car horn behind me beeped, and I jumped the two car lengths forward, then slammed on the brakes. I rolled down the window, stuck my head out, and turned around. "Are you happy now, huh? Are you happy?"

The guy behind me just shook his head in disgust. By the time we reached the customs booth, no one was crying. I looked at myself in the rearview mirror: my lip was still bleeding, and I sucked at it. Ellen's makeup was smeared. We couldn't be arrested for being unhappy, could we?

"Citizenship?" the young guard asked, bored, but slightly agitated.

"U.S. All of us."

"How long have you been in Canada, and for what reason?

"Camping at the Pinery. Just the weekend."

"Anything to declare."

"No. Nothing." I said without hesitation. The last time, two summers ago, I'd said "Just some dirty clothes," and had gotten a thin smile from the guard. "Nothing," I repeated.

"Okay, go ahead."

We drove up onto the bridge, where the traffic was already lightening, spreading out. I should have felt some relief, but there was none. I had told a lie in front of my sons. My wife had hit me. We'd given the boys enough lessons for one day. I wanted to toss the firecrackers off the bridge.

Everybody lies to their kids once in a while, but that's not the same as having them know you're lying, lying in a public way. I didn't care about the fireworks. That's what I thought to myself as we drove home. I knew something was wrong with my life if that was my idea of doing something for my kids. And if my gentle wife could slap me . . .

After we got home, the brick of fireworks just sat in the trunk of the car. The boys were probably afraid to even bring it up, as if those firecrackers were the lie itself.

■ ■ ■

In November, I asked for a demotion. It was the end of the line then as far as moving up the corporate ladder. I'd sawed off the next rung all by myself. I told the controller that my wife and kids needed me. He snorted. "We all got a wife and kids."

I tried to come up with additional reasons, trying to please him, to placate him enough so he wouldn't out-and-out fire me. "I'm not a leader, everyone knows," I said, "but I do good work." I pulled a roll of antacid tablets out of my jacket pocket and held them up. He countered by pulling a jug of liquid antacid out of his drawer. He slammed it on his desk. What made him different than me, I wondered.

"Well, Mooney, I don't think you're a coward," he said finally.

"Thanks," I said. He let me have my old job back. I moved my stuff back into my old cubicle, knowing I might never move again until I retired. On my desk next to a family picture, I placed a pic-

ture of me and Eddie Lovelock on a golf outing. I felt like that rac-
coon let out of the garbage can, but I didn't hiss at anybody. I just
sighed.

■　■　■

We didn't see Ken and Louise again for a long time. Ken and I never
had our talk, and I think we were both relieved about that. Ken's
work schedule was odd too. "The police station never closes," was
his pat response, though I could say the factory never closes, and
that too would be true. I think they must have heard what I'd said
outside that bathroom.

It's true, Ken was my only friend. I didn't count anyone from
work. Not since Lovelock died. Once I took his job, a lot of the guys
avoided me, either because I was the boss now, or because they
thought I'd be next to go down clutching my chest. After the demotion, I could never be one of the guys again. I was damaged goods—
no one wanted to get too close.

As for Ken and Louise, we used to comfort ourselves with their
kindness and friendship, but I don't think we gave much back.
Louise lived with the life-and-death uncertainty of a cop's wife, so I
think she was a little unsympathetic toward us and our problems. I
could just hear her telling Ellen, "Well, at least nobody's going to
shoot him."

Ellen didn't talk about Louise much after that weekend. Ellen
and I, overweight and spiritless, weren't a lot of fun to be around. I
knew I wasn't. Maybe it was just me, or maybe it was the job, or
both, but I hadn't felt much of anything in a long time.

■　■　■

I broke my news about taking the demotion at dinner one night—
dinner at the normal time. Ellen leaned over and kissed me.

"That's good," she said. The kids ate on in silence. "It means

Daddy's going to be home more often now," she said. "Right, honey?"

"Right," I said. I briefly closed my eyes and tried to imagine our future.

"Don't worry, we're still here," Ellen said.

After dinner, though it was cold and snowy and already dark, I asked the boys to come outside and help me with something. They groaned, but slowly bundled up and followed me out to the garage. I lifted the brick of firecrackers out of the trunk and carried it to the middle of the driveway.

"You're not gonna blow the whole thing up, are you?" Toby asked.

"Yeah, that was the idea," I said.

"You could at least blow something up with it," Brad said. "Let me go get one of my models or something." He ran in the house before I could answer.

Toby and I stood waiting in the cold. He pulled out a pack of matches.

"Where'd you get those?" I asked, slightly stunned by that casual gesture. "You smoking?" I asked him. Brad came running back out with a model of Dracula that he'd painstakingly painted just a couple of months earlier.

"You sure you want to blow this one up?" I asked. "You worked hard on it."

"I messed it all up," he said. I looked closely at the paint job as he handed it to me. Under the garage floodlight, it looked perfect.

I lit the master fuse, and we all backed up and stood side by side in the snow tracks my tires had made pulling in. The long series of explosions ripped through winter silence. Dark, plastic pieces of Dracula rained down onto the white snow. On the ground in front of us lay only firecracker shreds. The stinging smoke lingered. My ears rang with all the work to be done.

"I could have made fifty cents a pack on those," Toby said finally. I rubbed my numb hands together. Ellen had turned the porch light on, and so had some of the neighbors. Fireworks in November—I wondered how far the sound carried. Our next-door neighbor opened his door and shouted, "Is everything okay?" I know I should have answered him, but I didn't. "Is everybody okay?" he asked. I stood there with my boys. Nobody said a word.

Christmasmobile

Christmas Eve—which meant what? No school, for one thing. The first half of Ed's senior year at Fitzgerald High had not been what he'd hoped for. What had he wanted? A girlfriend, for one thing.

His old friend Sam was picking him up later. What were they going to do? That's what his parents would ask. When his father was off from the plant, he suddenly took an active interest in everything Ed did, as if he could make up for all the months when he was busy at work and didn't seem to care. The house was stuffy with holiday baking, everybody bumping against each other in the crowded kitchen. He slipped down into the basement, put on his earphones, cranked up some rock 'n' roll.

Even in the basement, he couldn't escape the season—Julie and Carl, his younger brother and sister, had hung red and green construction paper chains from the rafters. Ed didn't know how to act at Christmas. The excitement of being a kid and getting toys was long past. But he *wanted* to be excited—the build-up was so intense, it left Ed expecting some big thing, even though he *knew* no big thing was coming.

He'd done all his shopping two weeks earlier. He and Sam had sat in Sam's Impala in the Universal City Mall parking lot, drinking pints of Southern Comfort and eating penny pretzels, the engine running to keep them warm, to keep the battery charged for Sam's new tape deck. When they finally stumbled into the mall right before it closed, they bought the first things they saw. Getting drunk was a prelude to just about everything. One of Ed's classmates had told his mother, "Ed would be a decent guy if he wasn't so stoned all the time." His mother had told Ed what she'd heard, quivering through tears, but she had never told his father.

A voice was filtering through the *chachunka chunk* of the music. The high, sweet, frail voice of his mother. Ed took off the headphones. "Eddie, would you like to make some Christmas cookies with the other kids?"

His mother had no cookie cutters—everybody made their own shapes. He liked that about his mother—she didn't much like structure—though his father blamed Ed's bad behavior on that very thing. The King of Blame, Ed called his father. Whenever something went wrong, he was there with the pointing finger. Just yesterday morning, his father had come downstairs and found the power button of Ed's stereo left on and gravely gave him his "wasting electricity" lecture.

Should he make cookies, or not? His mother was waiting for an answer. "I'll be up in a minute," he said. Though it was hot and stuffy upstairs, the basement was cold. See what I mean? Ed said to himself, and clicked off the stereo. He checked again to make sure the red light was off.

■　■　■

Around seven o'clock, Ed heard a horn beep, a car idling in the street out front. He wasn't ready—it was early for Sam, but he knew it was him by the rumble of his exhaust system. Sam had tin-canned the exhaust pipe, but that barely muffled the noise. It was like the rumble of a cold deep in your chest. Ed quickly threw on his coat and headed for the door. His father sat in the living room, half-dozing through the TV news.

"Where you off to?"

Ed hadn't even thought of an excuse. "It's Christmas Eve," he said.

"Yeah?" his father said. "So?"

"We're gonna drive around . . . Look at the lights. Then . . . uh . . . we're going to midnight mass."

"Why don't you swing by and pick up your mother? I'm sure she'll want to go." His mother hadn't driven since she'd been in an accident five years ago.

Ed closed his eyes. His hand rested on the doorknob. "Dad, we might be taking some girls," he said. Talk about wishful thinking, he thought.

"What do you mean *might?*"

"I mean *might.*" Sam beeped his horn. Ed turned the knob. "I'll be home after mass," he said, and was out the door before his father could get in another word. It *was* Christmas Eve, and his father wouldn't stay mad at him tomorrow, even though Ed had gotten him another gadget—he'd grabbed a battery-operated shoe shiner from a pile of them near the entrance to Penney's.

Out in the fresh air, Ed rubbed his eyes and shook his head at the sight of Sam's Impala. It was decked out with blinking Christmas lights and silver tinsel, with a Santa head stuck on his antenna. Ed ran down the porch steps, jumped in, and slammed the door. The car reeked of pot, and Sam immediately handed him the joint he'd been smoking. "Merry Christmas, bro," he said.

"What the fuck?" said Ed. He couldn't get the grin off his face. He felt the weight of it hanging there. He didn't like to smile much, particularly at home. It was as if it was his job there to be sullen and unhappy, to bear a vague, general unhappiness he himself couldn't understand. He didn't know what would happen if he let his guard down, and he didn't want to find out.

"Welcome to the Christmasmobile—watch the wires on the floor, man."

Ed looked down. A nest of wires was plugged into the cigarette lighter. Sam was always working on his car. When it came to cars, he was The Man—he'd worked in his father's gas station since he was ten. Ed's father worked on the line at Chrysler's and had been talking about getting Ed a job there after he graduated. "That'll put an end to this nonsense," his father had said.

"Holy shit, Sam," Ed said. The lights blinked around the windshield, giving the dingy interior an eerie glow.

"You like?"

Ed took a long hit on the joint. "Fan-fucking-tastic . . . Man, I almost didn't get outta there. The old man was squawking at me. He wanted me to take my mom to midnight mass."

"Hey sure, why not? Light one up with the old lady on the way." They laughed. Ed loved Sam's big "har-dee-har-har." That laugh was his best feature. It filled the car with something sweeter than the smoke. Sam could laugh at anything. Everybody seemed to like him.

Ed himself was just a little shit, and he knew it. A smart-ass, a cartoon mouse who made a cruel joke, then snuck back into his little hole. He and Sam made quite a pair, a freak show no girl would get near. Ed had just about given up on growing any taller. He smoked as an excuse—"stunts your growth," he admitted at every opportunity. Sam was overweight, a threat to no one, and he had access to some of the best pot in the area. And he was generous with it—to a fault, Ed thought as he took a deep hit and Sam backed out into the icy street.

Ed looked up and saw his father standing behind the storm door, hands pressed against the glass. Sam pulled away, skidding a bit before gaining traction.

"Where to, my man?"

"Let's just cruise around and beep the horn at people," Ed said. And that's what they did. Everyone beeped back, even the police. Ed imagined the smiles in those dark cars. Sam was a fucking genius, he thought.

■　■　■

When Ed climbed up the stairs and entered the hot kitchen, Julie and Carl were already busy with their cookie trays, shaping the dough into their names, their dog Prince, their Christmas stockings, cars, the moon, and a whole series of blobs Ed could not distinguish. That was his specialty, he laughed to himself—blobs.

He overworked his dough till no one could tell what he'd made. Too many red hots, and they'd melt into a sticky blob. Or, too many jimmies. Or, the cookies melted into each other. They'd saved a seat for him. A tray of blank circles of dough sat ready to decorate. His mother was smiling, watching him—too carefully, he thought. The one who *was wasted all the time.* His mother's smile. What he wouldn't do for one of those smiles when he was a boy.

Now, she was after *him* to smile. She could still break him down sometimes. One night, she jumped off a chair to try to kiss him when he came out of the bathroom. He'd fallen back right through the cheap drywall. He and his mother laughed and laughed, conspiring on a story to tell his father when he got home while Ed wiped chalky plaster from his butt. Ed left the house and let his mother handle it. His father fixed the hole and never said a word.

Did it take knocking a hole in the wall to make him happy? Some days, he thought, it did. Today, his fingers in sticky dough, he forgot himself for a couple of hours. He ate most of his cookies while they were still warm, trying to destroy the evidence of his brief joy. He burned his tongue.

■ ■ ■

Sam and Ed sat in the church parking lot watching it fill up around them with the huge midnight mass crowd. Everybody was waving at them and shouting, "Hey, look at that." Sam had the engine running, the lights blinking. Ed turned the music down so they could hear the compliments.

At five to twelve, they guzzled their last beers and hurried across the street. The church was full, and the late arrivals had to stand in back—the swayers—party-goers who didn't want to get up and go to church hung over in the morning. Sam and Ed took their places back against the bare cement wall next to a couple older guys in leather jackets who had squeezed their dates into seats in the last row in front of them. The girls kept turning back and winking. These guys were cool, Ed thought. Clean-shaven, hair greased back, dressed in gray slacks and black dress shirts under their leather jackets—the dress uniform of all sophisticated toughs. Ed and Sam wore jeans and down jackets. Ed stuffed his new black gloves into his pockets and took off his stocking cap.

They stood silent during mass. A lot of the swayers, freed from the limits of the pews, were talking, a low buzz circling the rim of the round church. The girls stopped flirting. Ed stared at the backs of their heads, their shiny, flowing hair. He had never winked at a girl before. He'd been doing okay with girls back in junior high, when he didn't seem so short, but then everybody shot above him.

Carol Reinhart had kissed him at a party last month. Made out with him, actually. Minutes, they'd been kissing *minutes,* he told Sam. She was drunk, of course. So was Ed. She said he was cute. Then she patted him on the head. He hadn't told Sam that.

Ed looked around the church, spotting neighbors, kids from school. He was looking for cute girls, and there were a lot of them, dressed in their Christmas finest. He was keeping an eye out for his mother—maybe she'd gotten his father to take her after all, though he'd said he'd be too tired. Or maybe one of the neighbors had given her a lift. He didn't see her anywhere, though at the offering, Sam poked him. "Hey, your ma's here."

"Where?"

"Over on the other side." Sam started to point.

"Don't point," Ed said, pulling Sam's arm down. "I'll find her." He scanned each row but never spotted her.

Right before communion, a commotion arose in the middle aisle. A guy—Joe Radford's older brother—ran toward the altar shouting, "Bullshit, this is all bullshit!" He waved his arms. "Church is all bullshit!" Ed waited for him to say something else, but that was it. The ushers ran down and dragged him away. He put up a good fight and bloodied somebody's Christmas suit. Kicked out a window in a door on the way out.

"Holy shit," Sam said.

"You said it." Ed was shaking, as if *he'd* just uttered those words, put up that struggle. He could have—it was inside him to say that, to do something to disrupt the church's stuffy decorum. "Man, what's that guy on?"

"Some kinda bad shit," said Sam. "Let's get outta here."

Father Frank was trying to regroup down by the altar. He dropped the big prayer book with a thud. Somebody had fucked royally with the script, Ed thought, as he followed Sam out the side door. Sirens and flashers were approaching. Ed was worried they'd be mistaken for troublemakers, and he hurried to Sam's car, dancing impatiently as Sam lumbered over to unlock it.

"Of course it's all bullshit," said Sam pleasantly as he pulled out of the lot, "everybody knows that. Doesn't mean he's gotta kick out a window and mess up midnight mass for everybody."

"Man, did you see that look on Father Frank's face? It was priceless," Ed said. He thought Father Frank was a pious phony, always telling everybody what to do. What gave him the authority?

Memorizing a bunch of prayers didn't make you an authority on anything but the prayers.

"I wonder what pushed him over the edge?" Sam wondered, lighting up one more joint.

"What do you mean? He was stoned out of his fucking mind."

"So are we, but we're not going nuts on everybody. Must have been something. I mean, just think about it. He went right down the center aisle in the middle of mass in front of all those people. Something must have snapped."

"Yeah, I guess so," Ed said. When he was a kid, he'd had an attack of appendicitis in church, but was afraid to get up and walk out in the middle of mass. When he collapsed in his pew, they rushed him to the hospital, where he had an emergency appendectomy.

"Are you sure you saw my mom?" Ed asked. He didn't wait for an answer. "I hope she didn't walk—too fucking cold."

After church traffic thinned out, the roads were nearly empty. Fewer cars to beep at. Ed was tired, but he didn't want to go home. Sam was hungry, and they were looking for a place to stop, but everything was closed at one o'clock on Christmas morning.

"Wonder where Santa is right now?" Sam asked.

"Antarctica," Ed said.

"Long fucking way to go from there."

"Wonder how Rudolph got that red nose?"

Sam was the only one he could be this comfortable with, Ed thought, and that was only when they were stoned.

"Snorting too much coke," Sam said.

"You'll make a great Santa someday," Ed said. He meant it as a compliment. Sam had the round, red face for it, the playfulness.

"Yeah, and you'd make a great elf," Sam said.

"You got me there." Ed winced, and sat up a bit higher in the seat. He hadn't meant to make fun of Sam's weight.

Sam suddenly slammed on the brakes. The bright lights of Bray's Bellybuster were lit up, the Laughing Donkey revolving on the roof, oblivious to the season. Ed could see a few sad souls sitting at the counter through the glass walls.

"Hee Haw! Hee Haw! Looks like it's Bellybuster's," Sam said. He swerved into the parking lot. "Hey, you got any money?"

Ed had change from the twelve-pack they'd split earlier. "A few bucks."

"I threw all mine in the collection basket."

"Yeah, I saw that. What the hell were you thinking?"

"Everybody else was throwing in. It's Christmas. Hey, remember the time you put aluminum foil shaped like coins in your envelope?" Sam burst out laughing. "You always were a crazy little fuck."

Sam didn't know he'd turned in the aluminum foil not just once, but every week for months. "Yeah, and now I have to buy your burgers." They were called Bellybusters for good reason, and it wasn't the size, for the burgers were small, square, gray patties, only 39¢ each.

Sam ordered six burgers, and Ed four. "Merry fucking Christmas," Ed said to Sam as he paid for them.

Sam smiled. "Christmas spirit," he said, "you can't put a price on it . . . Windows or counter?" At the counter, you looked back into the stainless steel kitchen. By the windows, you stared at cars passing by on Eight Mile Road, the busy eight-laner that ran past auto plants and tool and die shops, bars and cheap restaurants.

"Counter," Ed said. "It's warmer." Two women sat at the counter, quietly sipping coffee. Dressed in micro miniskirts, long, teased hair darkly haloing faces bright with lurid makeup, they looked like zombie saints from planet sin. Sam and Ed joined them in awkward silence. Ed suddenly felt self-conscious about being alone with Sam on Christmas Eve. "Hey, is that your car out there with all the doo-dads on it?" the woman behind the counter asked. She was old enough to be their grandmother—gaunt, wrinkled, her stained uniform sagging over her rounded shoulders.

"Yeah," Sam smiled proudly.

"Ain't that illegal?" she asked.

"Lighten up, Babe, it's Christmas," a man said from the corner by the exit. Ed hadn't noticed him rigidly staring out into the night.

"I'm gonna lighten you up out of here in a minute," she said to him with harsh familiarity.

The man didn't move or respond. Ed turned back to the counter. The place was too small to talk without an audience. He wolfed the burgers down. He just wanted to go home now, but Sam was taking his time.

"Lovely evening, eh ladies?" Sam said.

Ed spit out his coffee and started laughing. Sam elbowed him in the ribs.

"Shouldn't you boys be home in bed waiting for Santa," one of them sighed, clearly tired herself.

"You obviously don't know who you're talking to," Sam said. "I am Santa Jr. In a few years, I'll be climbing down your chimney. Once the old man retires."

They all laughed, even the counter woman.

"Asshole," the other woman said, but she was smiling. Ed wasn't sure they were hookers, but he could see they were both definitely a lot older than what he'd first thought. The harsh, bright lights of the Bellybuster hid nothing.

And what did *we* look like, Ed wondered. Two teenage losers?

"And who are you, one of the elves?" the counter woman said to Ed, but nobody laughed, and he was quietly grateful.

When Sam finished his last burger, they got up to leave. "Ho Ho Ho, Merry Christmas, everybody," he said, and shook his belly, rustling his puffy down jacket.

"Yeah, yeah," the two women said, and waved them out the door.

When a car doesn't start on a cold winter night and you're not in your own driveway where you can shrug and head back in and deal with it in the morning, when it's 2:30 A.M., Christmas, and you're stoned and tired, that *whrr whrr whrr* of an engine not turning over is about the worst sound you could imagine.

Sam couldn't believe it, though he knew instantly the car wasn't going anywhere. "Shit, shit, shit," he said, and pounded on the steering wheel. Ed was already cold—he had been anticipating the warm blasts of heater air. They sat for a minute in the cold car underneath the donkey swirling in the sky above them. He held a burger and fries in his hooves. Ed noticed up close how the donkey's smile was more of a sneer.

They were a couple of miles from home, so they *could* walk. They couldn't imagine finding a tow truck to give them a jump anytime before morning.

"How about those hookers? Maybe they can give us a jump," Ed said. He looked around the parking lot: just one other car. Eight Mile Road was eerily quiet. Everything else in the world was closed. "You got your cables with you, don't you?"

"They're not hookers, man. You're just stoned. Of course I got my cables, think I'm an idiot?" He turned to the car. "Fucking Christmasmobile—how could you let me down?"

"So what makes you an expert on hookers all the sudden?" Ed said, but Sam was already pulling himself out of the car.

"Where's Santa when you need him?" Sam asked.

"Australia," Ed said. "Fucking Australia."

"You know, it's summer in Australia now."

The car, a late-model Oldsmobile Cutlass Supreme—not a bad looking ride, Ed thought—did indeed belong to the women. "See, I told you they're not hookers," Sam said under his breath as the women reluctantly followed them out into the cold.

"So, what kind of cars do hookers drive then?" Ed asked.

"They don't drive," Sam said, "they float." He was opening his trunk, where there were *no* jumper cables. Not even a spare tire. He'd taken everything out while he was crawling around the trunk wiring the Christmas lights.

The women had their own cables. They loaned them to Sam, then hurried back into the restaurant. Ed started up the Cutlass. It was plush and roomy. It smelled like sweet perfume and hair spray. Sam hooked up the cables, but his car still wouldn't start. He was humiliated into a stunned silence. The Christmas lights had done some kind of number on his electrical system.

"Well, we're ready to leave," one of the women said when Ed sheepishly handed her back the keys. The boys waited during a long pause while the women exchanged glances. "You live around here?" the other woman asked.

"Yeah," Sam said, staring down at the dirty snow.

"We'll give you boys a ride home. Your mommas are probably worried about you."

Sam and Ed sat together in the back. Ed felt like he had as a child in the backseat of his parents' old station wagon. The women said nothing except to ask for directions.

"Shit," Ed said suddenly, "I left my hat and gloves back there."

"Well, I ain't turning around for that," the driver said.

"No, no. I wouldn't ask you to," Ed said.

"Maybe they'll be there when we pick up the car," Sam said.

His new black gloves—he'd bought them for himself when shopping with Sam only to see his mother frown when she saw him wearing them. "Looks like I have to go back to the store," she'd said. "I got you some just like them." He'd liked how they made him feel—strong, powerful. He sheepishly hoped his mother hadn't returned the other pair.

The women dropped them off at a main intersection. Nobody

wished anybody a Merry Christmas. Ed and Sam shouted "thanks" as the Cutlass sped away.

The cold snow squeaked under their feet as they walked. "Man, getting picked up by hookers on Christmas Eve," Sam said finally. "That'll make a good story."

"Now they *are* hookers? You're fucking crazy," Ed said to him. "My fingers are gonna freeze off."

At the intersection where Ed's street met Sam's, they parted. "See ya tomorrow, bro," Sam said.

"Yeah. Later." After heading down the street a ways, Ed turned and shouted back to Sam, "Hey, it was a good idea—the Christmasmobile." Ed ran the rest of the way home, his cold breath exploding around him. It had been lightly snowing for hours, but before, it'd just been an accessory to their night. Now, it was all there was—pure white snow. Some houses had left their Christmas lights on, and the snow gently muffled the colors. Under the street-light on Ed's front lawn, the snow glowed peacefully on its way down. His were the only footprints on the street. The first footprints of Christmas morning. He looked back at the small indentations. His growth did seem stunted. When he stopped growing, would he stop *growing?*

The tree lights were on in Ed's house. Was it that late? Were his brothers and sisters already opening presents? The last few years, Ed had been sleeping in until nine or ten and missing the gift-opening chaos.

He turned up the driveway his father would make him shovel later. He had his own key, a present for his sixteenth birthday, and he opened the side door quietly, took off his shoes, and walked toward the bathroom. He peeked in the living room and saw his mother sitting in the dark, drink in hand.

"Merry Christmas, honey," she said to him softly.

"Mom, what are you doing up?"

"Oh, playing Santa Claus. Got a late start tonight. Your father conked out, so I had to do it myself. Come on in here . . . You can open a present if you want."

Ed walked into the living room. His eyes slowly adjusted to the dark, and he saw the array of gifts spread over the floor.

"Did you go to mass tonight?" Ed asked.

"Yeah," she sighed. "Yeah, I did . . . They'll be talking about that one for a long time."

"That's for sure," Ed said. "Hey, did . . . did you have to walk?"

"Yeah. Your dad fell asleep long before that."

"I'm sorry, Mom. We shoulda come by and got you." Ed's stomach was roiling with the cheap burgers, his own selfishness. "I'm really sorry."

"Oh, that's okay, honey. I needed the walk. The house gets pretty small and stuffy this time of year."

Through the soft glow of the lights, he peered at his mother, sunken into the recliner, nearly buried in her thick robe. Her voice sounded weak and weary. "Do you remember when you were in the hospital? I thought I was going to lose you that time."

"Aw, I wasn't that sick. Was I?"

"Yes, you were," his mother said flatly. "Did you know that boy?" she asked.

"He's a Radford."

"His poor parents."

"Yeah," Ed said. He wanted to say more, but he didn't know where to begin. "Did you take those gloves back?"

"Yes, honey, I did."

"I lost mine tonight."

"Maybe they'll be in lost and found at church."

"I doubt it." Ed could see the man in the corner of the Bellybuster moving to the counter and slipping them on.

"Some things never come back," she said, swallowing the last of her drink. Ed was still shivering. He rubbed his hands together, then pressed them against his numb ears.

"Where's my pile?" he asked suddenly. "Can I really open one?"

"Couldn't resist, could you?"

He saw his mother's teeth reflecting the soft colored lights. He'd gotten a smile from her, and he gave a smile back. It was all he had to give.

Sugar Water

"How about some sexy lingerie for a graduation present?" I said to
Sue. We were strolling past Victoria's Secret down at Universal City.

"Who was Victoria, and what was her secret?" Sue asked.

"You should know—you're the one in college . . . Probably some
queen who liked kinky sex."

"It's not kinky. It's classy. I shop there myself," Sue said, matter-
of-factly.

"I wouldn't know," I said. We'd been going out for six months
and still hadn't had sex. In our mid-twenties, we both still lived at
home. Most of my friends were married, and so were Sue's. She
worked as a secretary at the K-Mart headquarters down the road
from the mall while going to Wayne State at night, majoring in
social work. She was graduating at the end of summer term—just a
couple of weeks away.

My high school girlfriend had worked at K-Mart too—not at the
headquarters, but in the store, running a register. She was beautiful
and even modeled at the Auto Show once. She was runner-up for
homecoming queen—she lost because she didn't have enough

personality. Neither did I—not till I got drunk, but she didn't appreciate the personality I picked up after a few beers, loud and lurching, lurching and grabbing.

"It's good to have secrets," she said. "Life would be boring without them." She was always straightforward and honest. I couldn't imagine her with secrets.

"Hey, did you read the paper this morning?" I prided myself on keeping up with the outside world. At the Ford plant where I worked, the guys called me "The Professor" and often came to me for answers to questions about history, current events and shit. "Herschel Walker—you know, the football player?—he writes poetry. Can you believe it? This guy asked Herschel what he wrote about, and he said, 'Life. How we make it what it is.' What the hell does that mean?"

"That's why Herschel makes his money playing football," Sue said. That's what I liked about her. She could nail things down fast. I put my arm around her soft shoulder and squeezed, nuzzling her neck.

"You can't wait for anything," she said, pulling away with a smile. "You've got to be more patient." We were headed to the movies at the mall—our routine when we both had a day off. We usually caught a matinee or an early show. Sometimes we went out for drinks and dancing at night if I had a whole weekend off. Pretty ordinary, I guess.

■　■　■

I liked walking through the air-conditioned malls. I know some people complain how they're sterile and everything, but that's what I liked about them. The white benches, sparkling fountains. The clean, quiet streams of people passing slowly, headed someplace to spend their money and feel good about it. We'd usually stop in the bookstore. That was something Sue and I shared—she liked to read too. She thought I should go back to school, but she didn't understand that with the money I was making, there was just no going back. If I had to do what somebody told me, I wanted to get paid for it.

I was kind of a drunk in high school—like some of the girls were kind of pregnant. Somehow, I managed to get close to a B average, but I never considered college. It wasn't something my parents cared about, and none of my friends were going. After graduation, I worked at the Towne Club bottling plant down on Mound Road. First thing I did was go out and buy a Corvette—a used one, but it ate up my entire paycheck all the same. Next, I tried selling real estate—people always laugh when I tell them that. No one can imagine me doing it, and to be honest, I was horrible at it. I'd basically say, "Hey, check out this house. If you like it, let me know." My old buddy Tim still sells real estate, and he's doing great, but we're not such good friends anymore. It's not just because he's doing so well—the job changed his personality. It's like he can't turn off his sales pitch.

After the real estate fiasco, I was in the hole on car payments. I took a job in the plant with my dad to try to dig my way out. The plant was like this powerful magnet that sucked most of us in eventually. And a lot of the ones who pulled against its lure didn't end up any better off. You'd see them working the counter at the bowling alley or selling shoes at the mall, no happier than the guys at the plant, and poorer to boot.

While in school, I'd gone out and got drunk every weekend, and during the years since, not much had changed. At closing time down at the Tel-Star most Saturday nights, you'd find me sitting on a stool, yucking it up with some of my old pals. Until I ran into Sue. I think she wanted to save me from myself. Her dad was beyond saving, so she was coming after me.

■ ■ ■

We'd met on one of the few occasions I stepped inside a church in recent memory. It was Easter, the kind of sunny, spring day that makes you want to believe somebody could rise from the dead. I mean, brilliant—the grass turned green overnight, green and glowing under a big blue sky. Everything bright and innocent, like a new set of crayons or something. My mother was getting ready to go to mass, and on an impulse I said, "Wait. I'll go with you." I put on the suit from my real estate days, got my hair all wet and slicked back. She just smiled and shook her head as I held her arm and we walked to my car.

The church was decked out in Easter color. The grouch of a priest was still there from when I'd first stopped going to church ten years earlier, though even he seemed to lighten up a bit, in his phony, sentimental way. I spotted Sue across the church—sitting with her mother, just like I was. She wore a white jacket and red dress. I sat there trying to remember her name. She'd been a year ahead of me at Fitzgerald High, and we'd been in Personal Typing together. Don't ask me why I took typing. Or Electronics. Or Earth Science. Or Science Fiction. Or Music Appreciation. Or Auto Shop. Or Outdoor Chef. I was a floater during the years my high school was trying to get hip and offering courses that let you float. The one I didn't take was Drugs, Delinquency, and Disorder. That stuff, I already knew.

I wasn't even a C and E Catholic anymore—Christmas and Easter—so it was like going to a reunion. I saw a lot of old, familiar faces dotting the church, and I spent the entire mass trying to sort them out. The ushers were the same old guys. I tossed a dollar in the collection basket.

After mass, we blended into the joyful flow out the door. Our mothers knew each other from Meals on Wheels, where they were both volunteer drivers. They stopped on the sidewalk by the parking lot to talk. "Hey, don't I know you?" I said to Sue, circling around our mothers to reach her.

She smiled and squinted. The sun was behind me. "Weren't you the guy in my typing class at Fitz?"

I remembered why I took typing—to meet girls. I was the only guy in the class.

"Yeah, that was me," I said. "Doing any typing these days?"

"As a matter of fact, yes. Word processing. You?"

I looked at my hands and laughed. "No. I got this job where there's only two keys to press. Big keys. And I press them all day long, over and over."

"You're down at the plant," she said.

■　■　■

It's hard to explain, but going to the mall was like going to church. Compared to Ford's, it *was* church. It had a certain level of civility that I appreciated. People weren't cussing their heads off and grabbing their crotches and throwing around big chunks of metal. I was sober those afternoons, and, holding Sue's hand, I felt almost religious. She dressed nice. She wasn't the prettiest woman in the world, but she knew how to dress.

The plant was so greasy, they could never get anything clean. The guys in the cleaning department had the easiest jobs—they just wandered the aisles wheeling a mop bucket around, and no one expected anything from them. I dreamed of a job on the clean-up crew.

"You look nice today," I said, and I meant it. Sue had made some decision about us not sleeping together that I never understood. Looking back, I think it had something to do with trust. She knew she couldn't trust me. I brushed against her shiny white blouse and imagined the smooth skin beneath it.

"Compared to what you have to look at all day at work, a clean toilet probably looks nice to you."

A lot of women think I'm good looking. I'm not bragging. It just seems to be true. If I'm sitting with some guys, and there's a bunch of women sitting nearby, and if one of them is going to ask one of us to dance, it's usually me. It's the one thing I have in my favor, and it doesn't have anything to do with me as a person. I'm telling you this because you might be wondering what Sue saw in me. I think she saw a pretty good-looking unmarried guy around her own age. Sure, I've put on a bit around the middle, but no one would call me fat.

"Damn right," I said. "Clean toilets rate pretty high, but you . . . I'm serious, Jesus, Sue . . ." I said, and trailed off.

It was usually all downhill after the initial connection. I'm not as interesting as I look. Oh, somebody might be out to get laid, like me, and we end up in the sack and it'd be okay, more or less. But a real love relationship? I don't think I'd recognize that if it slapped me in the face.

In high school, I would have called her plain. Also, she seemed confident and self-assured, and that probably scared off a lot of guys. It scared me off back then—she wasn't one of the ones I flirted with in typing class. But at twenty-nine, I was beginning to want something besides good looks.

■　■　■

We sat in the car after a night of drinking, dancing. I could have used another beer, but I was trying to cut down, particularly when I was with Sue. We'd been necking like high school kids. In fact, we were parked where I'd always parked back then—Parkview, a short, dark side street where no one bothered you.

"I don't know what's wrong with me," she said, pulling away suddenly.

I tried not to bring up the subject of sex. We were adults, and Sue always made me conscious of that. I wanted to try to have an adult relationship where we talked seriously, where we were at ease with each other.

"What makes you think there's something wrong?"

"I just think . . . I wish I felt more physical. I feel like maybe I should have more desire—not just for you—I mean, for every-thing."

It seemed like her graduation was a deadline, like we had to decide something, or that something might be changed when she got her diploma. We were pressing much more than when we'd first gone out.

The windows were rolled down, and cool air slipped in against our skins as we sat apart. I didn't usually spit, but for some reason, I turned and spit out the window.

"Does that mean you want to go home?" I asked. I know that sounds lame, but I didn't know what to say to something big like that. I cared more about her than I had ever cared for anyone, which made me desire her even more, which made her refusal to have sex with me incredibly frustrating. I was more mixed-up than she was—I just couldn't talk about it.

She sighed, "I guess so."

When I pulled in front of her house, we could see the light from the TV from where we sat. It was around two in the morning.

"Ralph must be at it again," I said, "racking up the empties."

She pulled at her handle. "Call me," she said.

"I always do," I said. "I call you lots of things."

"I hate it when you dumb yourself down," she said. She shook her head and got out. I blew her a kiss.

"Missed me," she said, and walked away.

■　■　■

Sue's family was planning a big graduation party. In our neighbor-hood, you had a high school graduation party because everybody knew you'd be going no further. If somebody actually graduated from college and then had a party to boot, that'd be like rubbing it in. But Sue was special—she'd done it on her own, taking eight years, and no one begrudged her the party.

Everybody had a garage behind their houses, so looking over the fences, you could see what looked like big boxcars, identical, trailing off down the tracks of our lives, the tracks that led past the old abandoned shopping center down to the mall, past the church, the high school, and down to the plant.

I'd switched my work schedule and gave up Sunday double-time so I'd be off for her party.

■　■　■

"Social work—what do you do with that?"

We were passing Spencer Gifts and Just Lamps.

"You try and help people. Don't you think there are a lot of people who need help around Detroit?"

I laughed. "Yeah, but who pays you to help them? Isn't that one of the lowest paying fields?" I'd read that somewhere.

"Why is it always money with you?"

"Well, I mean, why go to college and everything if you're not gonna make more money?"

"You sound like my dad."

I probably did. I didn't want to end up there, where her dad was, drinking himself into oblivion in front of the TV every night. Maybe somebody like Sue could help me get my act together. And, after all, I did read. I was paying attention, I told myself.

■　■　■

My father had died two years earlier—he never believed in any of that insurance crap. He was big into credit cards—he thought that was reverse insurance—they were assuming you'd live long enough to pay off your bills. My dad, he had a lot of theories. He always encouraged me to read. He liked to read about the great inventors.

Nikola Tesla was his favorite. "Fuck Thomas Edison," he'd say. "Fuck Henry Ford. Tesla could kick both their asses."

He was always coming up with ideas for the suggestion program at the plant—a Ford axle plant. One time he won a thousand dollars. That might have been the proudest moment in his life. Mostly, he won little flashlights or coffee mugs.

After he died, I lost it for awhile. I was waking up in rundown hotels, or on somebody's couch, or in strange apartments with women whose names I didn't pretend to remember. I started showing up late for work, and my foreman gave me a warning. "An idiot could do your job," he said, and he was right. I had a system which let me sneak away two hours every day to sleep on a bed of cardboard hidden in a storage area. I was a smart guy. A lot of people said, "You should be in college. What are you doing here?"

"College?" I'd say. "And study what?"

Sue thought she was helping me get it back, whatever it was I'd lost, and maybe she was. I was thinking about things more, even if it was simply to argue against her insistence that I look at the big picture of my life. She kept trying to get me to take a class at the community college. "Just one class," she'd say. "Just to see."

My mother didn't bother me after my father died. I was paying the mortgage, and I was an adult. She didn't nag me about when I came and went. I think she was hoping I wouldn't get married, at least until the house was paid off—four more years. She liked Sue, though. She said to me once, "Wouldn't it be nice if you ended up with a college girl like Sue with a head on her shoulders." My mother thought it was a novelty for me to go out with somebody who had a brain.

■ ■ ■

I'd been ripping the cheap paper tablecloth into long strips. The bottoms of my beer bottles were sweating wet circles through the paper. Old Milwaukee. Sitting in the shade of the garage, I could still feel the day heating up. I hated Old Mils, but at least they were ice cold. A big bucket of ice in the corner of the garage was stuffed with beer and those cheap flavored pops from Towne Club made especially for occasions like this at $4.99 a case.

I was sitting with Sue's old high school friend, Karen. Sue was busy greeting relatives and trying to keep her dad from getting too loaded too early in the day. I felt Karen's long bare leg smooth against mine. She wore a short jean skirt and tight black blouse. Her blond hair shone bright in the dim, oil-stained garage. I felt pale, washed out. I was drinking fast, nervous with all Sue's family there. It was just a garage party, but I still felt self-conscious, and a little depressed. Okay, a little jealous too.

The first college graduate in her family. Big doings. Two doors down, they were having a communion party. A bored little girl in a white dress stared at us through the fence. They had Michelob down there, I could see, and hardly anybody drinking. Maybe it was too early. Not for me. Not at this party. Sue wore a green pantsuit and white shoes. She was looking over at me. I gave a little wave.

Karen and I were talking about famous high school parties it turned out we'd both been at. I didn't really know her and Sue back then. They were a year ahead of me when a year was a hundred miles, another time zone. Now, it was right next door. Karen was single too, and living at home with her divorced mother. I heard a woman's loud, piercing laugh from the backyard.

Karen rolled her eyes. "That's my mother—what's she doing out there?"

I poked my head around the corner of the garage. "I think she's trying to stab somebody with a lawn dart." I liked Karen—she had a danger sign tattooed on her forehead, where sweat glistened beneath her hairline. I impulsively reached under the table and squeezed her knee.

Sue's dad was wrestling with a big boom box. Somebody wanted the ballgame on. It was the kind of party I'd been going to all my life. But every so often, somebody seemed to be looking at me, or pointing discreetly at me. Was I being called "the boyfriend"? Sue'd told me that some of her family thought she should be married by now.

■ ■ ■

"I don't know if I ever want to get married," Sue told me one night.

"Right," I said. "Every one of my married friends said that, then they met somebody, and *boom.*"

"No, really. I don't think I've ever felt *boom* before. It's like there's some kind of filter between me and the world. Nothing can penetrate."

"I feel that way sometimes too," I said.

"Yeah?"

"Yeah, that's when I go out and get really drunk."

"That just makes the filter thicker," she said.

"Yeah," I said, "but the hangovers sure penetrate."

"You're going to end up like my dad," she said with what sounded like both bitterness and disappointment. "You're right behind him, you know." Sue'd been trying to get her father into treatment. The union would pay, but he wouldn't go.

I hated it when she compared me to her dad. I was just a young guy who liked to get loaded now and then. I never drank alone, like her dad did. He worked at the plant too—on days. He knew my type. I think he used to be my type until he got tired. I never wanted to get tired, tired like that.

She seemed depressed. "I'm thinking about going back into real estate," I said. That always cracked her up.

■ ■ ■

I'd choked on the idea of a gift. Nothing seemed to send the proper message. I didn't know what the proper message was. I'd wandered around the mall in a daze, leaving with one of those stupid Studio cards that were supposed to be funny but never quite were. I wrote a note inside that promised to take her out to celebrate.

It was a bright Sunday in August with almost enough breeze to make you forget your shitty job—excuse me, *my* shitty job—which was tossing axle housings onto pallets. I was on a waiting list to get into skilled trades, though since I didn't jump into the plant straight from high school, a lot of guys were ahead of me.

Karen and I were sitting close now, our legs meshed beneath the table. She was burning up, and I was too. Time was stretching out, the afternoon sliding into a blur. Those tablecloths didn't hide much. I glanced over and saw Sue's dad give me a "I'd kill you right now but I'm not gonna ruin my daughter's graduation party so you'd better get the hell out of here" look. Sue was nowhere in sight. I got the message.

"Let's get out of here," I said. Karen guzzled her Old Mil.

"Good beer, eh?" she said.

"Get out," I said. "It's shitty beer."

"It's cold, sucker—drink up."

I smiled wide. That was my kind of talk. I felt reckless and giddily stupid. I got to my feet, and Karen and I walked out of the backyard, a few stares nudging us down the driveway. I thought about Sue—I did—but lust was eating me up.

■　■　■

The neighborhood was quiet that Sunday afternoon. A bored couple on their porch, the man waving a hose over thin scraggly bushes, his wife inhaling deep on a cigarette. Karen wrapped an arm around my waist as we searched for somewhere that wasn't so bright. We were exposed now, and the beer was making me sleepy. We turned the corner, and in the distance I saw the tiny park where I used to buy drugs as a teenager. We picked up the pace. Maybe Karen had bought her drugs there too. We weren't saying much. It was one of those animal things—lust, pure lust, and neither of us wanted to spoil it.

■ ■ ■

Everybody had been asking Sue what her plans were, as if graduating from college suddenly entitled you to have plans. She'd told me she might have to take a pay cut to go into social work. "There's nothing wrong with staying on at K-Mart," I said, but she'd given her notice there, and she wasn't looking back. She'd be unemployed in a couple of weeks, and everybody was asking "what are your plans," like she was going to be president some day.

What were *my* plans? I had none, and Karen wasn't interested in hearing them even if I did. We hurried to the back of the park where some clustered trees blocked the view from the road. She pushed me back against one of those trees, and we started kissing, her mouth and tongue, a wet, hot cleansing machine, like the spray gun that cleaned the presses at the plant. I reached behind her and squeezed her ass through her jean skirt. She pushed herself into me. I ran my hands up under her blouse and quickly unsnapped her bra. She crammed a hand down my pants and grabbed me. I slipped a finger under her panties. She gasped. I moaned. It was a wet smeary blur as we went at it, tumbling onto the grass and weeds, rolling over the big roots. She kicked off her panties and hiked her skirt over her hips. "Put something besides your finger in there," she said, and I did.

Somebody whistled from the street. We didn't look up. "Hey," somebody shouted. We didn't look up.

I wanted to lie there with her forever, exposed in Toepfer Park— but the drug dealers and wine drinkers would be showing up soon, and this was their spot. We put ourselves back together in silence. We stood and walked out of the park, wandering aimlessly down one street, then the next, dizzy with what we'd done.

Karen and Sue were friends going back to grade school. My car was parked at Sue's, and I knew I had to go back there to get it. Suddenly, Karen stopped. "This is my house," she said, and turned toward me.

"Well," she said.

"I'd sure like to see you again," I said.

"That might be hard," she said. I squeezed my eyes shut, then opened them again.

"Can't I call you?" I asked.

"How about I call you?" she said. I wasn't sure if she ever would, but I quickly gave her my number.

"Aren't you going to write it down?" I said. I was beginning to feel like this was a blow-off. I'd done the same thing enough times myself.

"I'll remember," she said, and repeated the number, then walked up the sidewalk and into her house.

I kept walking. This wasn't exactly my neighborhood, but I knew it well enough from high school nights of aimless cruising and drinking. Did I do something wrong? I wondered. Too fast? I tried to go over the sex, but it was a hot rush, like a bee sting—it lingered, but what could I remember? It was muggy now, early evening, hazy, the sun reluctant about going anywhere. I smelled her on my fingers. I felt my sweat mixed with her sweat. I circled back past her house like a dog, but I didn't stop.

It was getting dark by the time I found myself in front of Sue's again. Sue. Shit. I felt a deep ache, and shame. I'd fucked up, big time. The party was over, and her father's car was gone. I walked up the driveway. A few Towne Club bottles still floated in melted ice. Looked like Fruit Punch and Lime—nobody liked those flavors.

I knocked softly, and Sue came to the back door and stood for a while without saying anything. Her mother came up behind her, but Sue waved her away.

"I'm sorry," I said. She opened the door and stepped onto the stoop under the dim yellow porch light.

"You take off with my oldest friend, and that's all you can say?"

I took a step back from her, thinking she could smell the sex on me.

"We just went for a walk," I said.

"Yeah, right. I know Karen. I know you. Why? Why did you embarrass me like that?"

She seemed pretty calm, considering. I almost wished she was more angry. I wanted everyone to care a little more about what had happened, including myself.

"Well, what do you want? Why are you here now?"

That was an adult question. I shrugged like an idiot. I wasn't sure. After a long, awkward silence, she stepped inside and turned off the porch light. She stood looking out at me through the screen.

"You can't have it both ways," she said.

I was too tired and hung over to read her expression in the darkness. I wasn't sure what she meant, but I said, "I know, you're right. Look, I'm sorry." I turned and walked away to my car. She wasn't stopping me.

■　■　■

Karen did call me, once, two months later. We went to a movie at the mall and necked in the seats, then we went back to her house and had sex. No one was home. Her mother was out on a date herself, and Karen didn't seem concerned about her showing up while I was there.

It turned out Karen had a serious boyfriend.

"How serious?"

"We're engaged," she said. "It looks like we're getting married." She opened the closet and pulled out a wedding dress.

"Wow," I said. "It looks like you are."

"He's a computer programmer," she said.

"Yeah, me too." I joked.

She laughed. The sex hadn't been nearly so good or interesting in a bed after a date.

"Getting it while you can, eh?"

"You bet," she said. "Hey, you know, you should call Sue back. We talked. She's cool about everything. You give yourself too much credit. It's not like you broke her heart—you just embarrassed her."

"We did," I said. "Both of us." A noisy, persistent bird was chirping on the telephone wire out front, though it was still dark out. The sound echoed off the silent street. I knew it was time to go.

When I left Karen's, the garbage truck out front was having engine trouble, and the garbagemen were cursing. Karen and I kissed at the door. I tried to pull her lips into mine, but she backed away, and I never saw her again.

■ ■ ■

At Towne Club, I worked bottling that sugar water—lugging empty wooden cases, washing the returned bottles, filling them again, the colors rising obscenely bright into the necks as if those bottles had never been used before. They didn't care how it tasted, as long as the colors were bright. There was a rumor somebody found a rat in a bottle of orange soda. Must've been a pretty small rat. I saw Davey Reed try to squeeze a tiny mouse in a bottle, but he couldn't do it.

Karen was a Towne Club kind of girl, and I was the kind of guy fooled by bright colors. That plant's closed now, but you can see cases of empties stacked up in the grimy windows, probably still sticky with spit and sugar, waiting for the washer.

I should probably tell you, the kind of books I read aren't going to make me a scholar. Mysteries, detective stuff. Have you read any of these books about this detective named Lazlo? They're my favorites. Lazlo always gets his man and gets the girl too. I like the silence of entering another world. Flipping the pages late at night, alone. Or even at work in the middle of all that noise, I can get away. I read about smart people who figure things out and know the right things to say. In other words, fantasy.

One thing I don't like about the mall is the food court. It seems too much like the satellite cafeterias in the plant. Sure, you've got more choices. But I've never seen anybody say, "Wow, this is great. I just love the food here. And the atmosphere!" You're sitting there at these rickety tables in the middle of nowhere. Not that I'd know quality if it punched me in the nose.

The little first communion girl in the white dress didn't look like she was having any fun. Envelopes full of money didn't mean much to her yet, but they would. The money was going straight into a bank account, maybe not even her own. At least, that's how it was for me. I did get a prayer book from my grandmother. In high school, I cut the pages out of it to hide my dope in. That's the kind of guy I was. The kind of guy I still am? I keep trying to figure that out.

"A red Corvette? Isn't that kind of a cliché?" Sue said to me the first time I took her out.

That stung a little. "But it's my kind of cliché," I said, trying to laugh while my face flushed. I always liked eight cylinders, even during the gas crunch. I liked the quick pick-up when I touched the gas.

I never saw Sue again either, and it's my loss. Maybe she was too smart for me, though it'd get her mad, my saying that. I didn't want to work hard enough to figure her out. It is true that sometimes I feel the world is filtered by something, and I can't penetrate enough to get beyond the cheap joke, the easy laugh. Maybe it's the factory work—I can't stop the repetitive gesture.

I drove by Sue's house again that night after the party. The lights were all off. And then I drove by Karen's again. Dark too. Then, I sped off, my foot to the floor. My whole life seems like it's been one quick fix. Maybe I'm destined to drive by the houses of women all the nights of my life, wondering what's inside. I turned right, I turned left. I know these streets, how one flows into another, circles back.

The Jimmy Stewart Story

No, not that Jimmy Stewart. A lot of people think Jimmy Stewart was a great guy, with his sappy poems about his pets, his "Aw, shucks," routine. But he had a dark side, like in *Rear Window,* spying on his neighbors. That's the Jimmy Stewart I'm like. Everyone thinks ministers are harmless, without ambition, without problems, some kind of junior angels designated by God. I have my dark side, and I make no apology for it. And if I do say so myself, I could write the pants off Jimmy Stewart.

Why don't I go by James or Jim? People make the connection regardless, so I just deal with it head on. That's what first attracted me to Elizabeth Taylor. On the first day of my high school Bible study class, I asked the students to introduce themselves. Cindy, Bill, Toby, etc., then, "Elizabeth Taylor." Not just Elizabeth, not Liz, not Beth. Some of the students stared, almost as if she *was* Elizabeth Taylor. After a few snickers, a few titters and whispers, we continued. No one else said their last name.

I should be up front about a few things: Liz is black, and I'm white. She was seventeen then. The congregation is about 80 percent white, 20 percent black. I'm married, and my wife Helen and I have two sons. I did not have an affair with Elizabeth Taylor. I am no longer a minister.

Ministers, teachers, parents—all inevitably have favorites, and Liz was mine, I freely admit. And I think I filled a need in her life at the time. The previous summer, her father had died in an accident at the Chrysler plant—a forklift pinned him against a wall and crushed his chest. She and her mother moved in with her grandmother, a member of my congregation.

I never asked if they named her after the actress. We named one of our sons Albert, and it turned out there was a pop singer years ago named Al Stewart who had one hit album, *The Year of the Cat.* My friend Joe from the seminary sent it to me as a joke after receiving the birth announcement. It's not like naming a child "Penny Coin" or something—no gimmick, just coincidence. That's what my mother said, but all the same, she was a big Jimmy Stewart fan and watched *It's a Wonderful Life* more than any reasonable person should.

■ ■ ■

—*Why did Judas betray Jesus?*
—*He was too Peter-ed out.*

Liz asked questions others were afraid to ask:
  "Was there really an Adam and Eve?"
  "Where was the Garden of Eden?"
  "Was Jesus white or black?"
  "How come Catholics have communion all the time and we only have it once in a while?"
  "How would Jesus like you making jokes about him?"
  I came to eagerly anticipate the weekly challenge, the questions I could never quite answer to Liz's satisfaction—a little game we played at the end of class.

Then, one day: "Rev. Stewart, is there sex in heaven?"

The room exploded into shouts and laughter. While I waited for calm, I tried to think of an answer.

"No one's exactly sure what heaven's like . . . Or at least no one has come back and told us." (More laughter.) "Though people do tell us what sex is like, and some of them say it's like heaven." A few nervous giggles.

"I don't think there is," she said. "Because if there was, then women could have babies in heaven, and that doesn't make sense because you have to be on earth before you get to heaven. You have to *earn* heaven."

My face flushed. The room was always stuffy, but it seemed particularly hot that afternoon, one of those surprisingly warm days in spring when the furnace doesn't catch on fast enough to shut itself off. "Maybe you can see me after class, and we can talk about this privately." I had just wanted to stop the discussion, but I knew immediately I'd said the wrong thing. The air turned quiet and threatening. I heard a few snickers. "Any other questions?"

No, not after that. I was hoping she'd simply go away, but she sat on the radiator waiting for me at the back of the classroom as I gathered my things, and a few heads turned to take note as they filed out the door.

"Yes, Liz," I said. "Now, what else can I . . . What more . . ." I couldn't figure out how to begin a discussion I wanted over as soon as possible.

"Rev. Stewart, I just don't understand what happens when we die."

I smiled. Death, I could handle. "Well, it depends on how you've lived your life."

"I know about sinning," she waved at me urgently. "I want to know what heaven's like. What's my father doing?" She got off the radiator and took a few steps toward me.

"Again, we're not sure, but it's a place where you'll be in the presence of God. You won't be burdened with the struggles we have on earth. Your father should be at peace."

"I tell you where he should be, he should be right here helping me out. My mom's always working, and my grandma's—well, you know my grandma. I don't have any brothers or sisters, and I don't think I'll be getting any now. The boys don't want to talk about anything serious, and the girls neither. You're the only one talks to me serious."

Her eyes flashed. Her intensity overwhelmed any analysis, any subtle nuance of emotion.

"Liz," I said. "Your father did not choose to die. God took him, like he'll take us all. You'll make yourself crazy trying to figure out why who dies when. I grew up without a father too. The important thing . . . the important thing . . ." Liz was beautiful. Her skin had the warm sheen of the new season. I trailed off.

Being a minister put a barrier around me. People couldn't seem to act natural in my presence. I always wanted to say, "Hey, lighten up, I'm just a normal guy." But I was connected to God, and they couldn't forget it. It was difficult to make any real friends. I rarely had a chance to visit other ministers, and with most of them, I couldn't be completely straight, couldn't admit to feelings I wasn't supposed to have—like my feelings for Liz. When she talked to me, she did not take on phony piety or deference. I know, I know, she was just a kid. Rationally, it was all wrong. Morally too.

She snapped her fingers in my face. "Hey Rev., snap out of it."

I shifted into automatic pilot: "The important thing is that you continue to live a good life in the face of these challenges. In God's wisdom, he has chosen to make your life difficult at this point. You must trust in the Lord."

She shook her head and frowned, repeating, "Hey Rev., snap out of it."

I just smiled nervously and shrugged, straightening desks that didn't need straightening.

When I looked up again, she stared into my eyes. I paused. "Do you understand the concept of faith?" I asked. "Seriously."

"I understand love. Faith is too far out there."

"Well, we have to have faith that God will reward us for leading a good life here, in this world. You have to trust God." I'd spent many long nights struggling with my own faith, with the question of what constitutes a good life. "What happens when we die? You can dress it up and talk about heaven and hell, but finally, no one really knows. I think we all struggle with the big questions, whether we realize it or not. Even faith in God doesn't answer them all, doesn't satisfy us here where we want the answers, where we want to *know*."

She smiled. I thought our discussion might be over, but after a moment, she continued, "I bet my daddy's bored out of his mind up in heaven, without the struggles . . . I mean, I *like* some of the struggles here—trying to run fast in track, studying for school . . . And I like kissing boys and all that . . . My grandmother, she tells me being with boys leads to trouble. That I shouldn't, that I should save myself . . . you know . . . Nobody waits till they're married anymore . . . Did you, Reverend Stewart?"

I wished I was home with my wife and kids. At least part of me did. "You should wait until you're emotionally committed to your partner," I said. "Yes, the facts are that a majority of people in this country have sex before marriage. That doesn't make it right . . . It's complicated."

"Yeah, I know. That's why I'm asking. Did you wait?"

Suddenly she was standing close to me. I looked around the empty room, took a step back. "That's a personal question."

"We're having a personal conversation, aren't we?" She gave me a little smile and moved still closer. Something heavy yet hollow sat in the pit of my stomach: she was flirting with me. I was aroused, I admit. Her hair was pulled back to reveal the perfect oval of her face, her large, bright eyes. Her dark skin shone through her thin white blouse. I asked God to help me. I tried to picture my family, my two beautiful kids. But they were blurred by the sexual haze hanging in that stuffy room.

"I'll never tell," I said, and smiled. My hands were shaking. I put them on her shoulders. "Maybe you should talk to a counselor at school about this. A woman. Get a woman's perspective."

She rolled her eyes. "You're going to cop out on me, aren't you?" She put her thin hands on top of mine. I knew I should have pulled away. She held them briefly, and we were suspended there. A minister is God's representative and cannot abuse that responsibility. But Liz wasn't thinking about God, and neither was I. We embraced, my arms circling her clumsily. I heard a noise somewhere and quickly pulled away. Or we both did.

"I think it's time to get you home."

"Time for something," she mumbled. She turned around. "It's dark out."

"I . . . I'll drive you." I closed my eyes and took a deep breath.

We rode much of the way in silence as she sat slouched against the passenger door. When we eased to a stop outside her house, I said, "Sex between two people who love each other is not a sin. Sex is a natural process, and there's no sin in enjoying it . . ." I knew I'd blown it earlier, getting flustered. Relieved and disappointed both. Here, in the open, on the street, I could be, needed to be, the minister again. But she had let me be someone else entirely, and I needed that too.

"Birds do it, bees do it, even monkeys in the trees do it," I sang. "Listen, Elizabeth, we can't imagine the pleasures of heaven. Just focus on this life here. Don't worry about what happens next . . ."

"I know," she said, " 'have faith.' " She pulled on the door handle.

She squeezed my thigh close to the groin. My mouth opened, but she quickly slipped out the door.

The answer was yes, I did have sex before I married. Helen wasn't the first, but she was the only one after I was ordained. Kelly Hunter is the one I remember the most. It was primal and direct with her. I felt I was in touch with pure flesh—nothing mental, nothing spiritual. Sex with Helen was tense and quiet. We never had the animal lust. The attraction was there, but it was the attraction of two match heads.

I drove home, troubled, dazzled, by that close brush with . . . with *something.* I circled the block twice before pulling in the driveway.

My sermon that Sunday was titled, "You Have to Earn Heaven."

■　■　■

—What did the minister say at Frankenstein's funeral?
—Rest in pieces.

Some of my classmates at the seminary told dramatic stories of what led them to the ministry—a major crisis, a moment of revelation, an inspiring mentor—but I think some of them became ministers because they didn't fit in with the rest of the world. They couldn't talk about sin in a convincing way—not enough experience. It's like a Catholic priest talking about marriage. How could he begin to know? Joe and I and a couple other seminarians used to go out for nights of what we called Sin Research—drinking, dancing, chasing women. I don't think we were really "sinning" on those nights. I think God wants us to have some fun. As long as it doesn't hurt others.

One of my favorite Bible stories is the Wedding at Cana where Jesus turns water into wine. Some argue that it's inconsistent with the rest of Jesus' life, but I like that Jesus—fun-loving, wanting the party to go on.

Why did I sign on? I needed Jesus, and I wanted Jesus to need me too. Maybe I became a minister because I couldn't cope either—couldn't cope with how unfair life seemed. How easily one man took another's life, whether on the street, or on the battlefield. I thought about the Peace Corps, or Vista, but I wanted more God in it. I wanted to help people spiritually.

My father left my mother when I was four. I barely remember him and have never tried to track him down. I grew up in the projects in Detroit. My mother worked as a secretary, and we managed—I suppose it was tough, though not unbearably so. One drunken teenage night, I came home with a tattoo. Luckily, it is hidden—on my back—and is not obscene.

My mother had raised me in the faith, but I'd drifted away during high school. It didn't help that our minister at that time supported the war—the Vietnam War. Detroit had burned in the riots of 1967, and my friendships with the blacks in the projects burned up too. It seemed like the world had no moral center. I needed, and still need, something at the center. If He's not at the center, then what do we have? Chaos. Selfishness and evil.

I swore I'd never turn anyone away from the faith. When I signed on, people were leaving in droves, young people, disillusioned with the rigidity and hypocrisy they saw in organized religion. And the people who *were* going to church were either going to black churches or white churches. I thought that if we all came back, if we united under one roof, we could make church a better place, remake it into *our* kind of church.

■　　■　　■

—*Ch__ch. What's missing?*
—*YoU aRe.*

Every congregation seems to have its "holier than thou" element, and mine was no different. Unfortunately, these men and women usually serve on church councils. They're like the kids who squeal on you if you talk while the teacher's out of the room. They want to be good so bad that they point out the badness in others every chance they get. That might sound bitter, but I won't take it back.

My church was on the edge of Detroit, and back in the fifties, the neighborhoods of my congregation had originally consisted of white working-class families. Now that those people were older, their children had grown up and moved out into the suburbs. What I was left with were older white couples and younger black families. Two of the older white men from the church council, Milton and Craig, came to me on a Saturday afternoon while Helen was out with the kids.

Milton was a local barber who owned two shops and offered the cheapest haircuts in town. It bothered him that I'd gotten my haircut there once, then never returned. It was a bad haircut—there's no rule that says you have to get bad haircuts to be a good minister. I favored the free-spirit, hair-over-the-collar peace-lover look. I think he had Friar Tuck in mind. He cut it so I looked like Moe from the Three Stooges. My hair offended him, and he was trying to put me in my place. He didn't charge me—as if he was doing me a favor. I like to look good. Is that a sin?

"Reverend Stewart, we've heard stories about you and one of the girls in Bible study, and we'd like to hear your side before we proceed," Craig said between his thin, pursed lips. They stood awkwardly on the porch. Not "to decide whether to proceed," but "before we proceed."

"What?" I stood squeezing the doorknob. I knew instantly that they meant Elizabeth Taylor. I kept them standing on the porch, the screen between us. "I don't understand."

"We heard you're getting too friendly with one of the colored girls," Milton chimed in, almost chirpy. Craig frowned, quickly adding, "One of the *black* girls." Craig was a Sunday school teacher and funeral home director, and he had no sense of humor whatsoever. He smoked stinky cigars, so I stopped riding to the cemetery with him. Another snub.

"In eight years," I began, "I've never had any trouble here. I can't imagine what the trouble could be now."

"The kids say you gave some private sex-ed to that girl," said Craig. Milton stood behind him salivating. I've never blamed the kids, who, after all, were at the age when sex was a major preoccupation. I believe they meant no harm. They didn't understand how this kind of talk changes once adults get a hold of it.

"How did you two get picked to do the questioning?" I asked. "Let me guess, you volunteered?"

"That's right," Craig said. "We're here to do our jobs as duly elected representatives of the church council. We have evidence . . ."

"What is this, a witch hunt?" I asked.

"What this is is long overdue," Milton said. " Look, we know she asked about sex in class, and you invited her to stay after . . ."

"Look, I didn't . . ." I began.

Milton continued, "invited her to stay after class, were seen driving her home that night. It wasn't the first time she'd stayed after class. The other kids say she's your pet."

"This is insane. I can explain . . . She was confused about the distinctions between the physical and sexual—I mean, spiritual and—physical and spiritual worlds, and I tried to clarify them for her." Milton snickered, but I continued, "I see nothing wrong with that. Absolutely nothing . . . The girl has no father."

"Right," Craig said, "and who was trying to take advantage of that?"

"As a minister, I have always considered myself above suspicion when it comes to being seen alone with a woman, or driving a student home. It was dark when Elizabeth and I finished talking, and I thought it only right to drive her home."

"We want to hear your specific memories of the conversation, and what took place afterward, beginning when class ended. We have witnesses to everything before that," Milton said.

"What do you mean, 'Everything before that'? It was just a normal class . . . I'm a minister. Just what am I being accused of?"

"This is about God," Milton said, out of nowhere.

"If this was about God . . . If this was about God, I could explain . . . You two . . . Everything I did . . . I . . . What is it, exactly, that you want from me?"

"We believe our spiritual leader should be above reproach, not mooning after high school girls."

"Here's my statement: I didn't have sex with her."

"We didn't ask you if you did," Milton said. "Now, do you want to tell us what you *did* do with her?"

"We talked."

Craig took over. "Maybe you'd like to resign. Make it easy on yourself."

"Make it easy for *you,* you mean. This is my life you're talking about. This isn't just some, some *job!*"

"We're paying your salary . . . We're paying your rent."

"Me and you, Reverend Stewart, we got different Gods," Milton said, shaking his head.

"Ain't it the truth, Brother Milton." I slammed the door on them.

That night after dinner, I sent Al and Frank out to play in the yard. We could see them out the window chasing each other.

"Helen," I said, "please sit down."

"What is it?" She was sweeping crumbs off the table into her hand. Maybe she had heard some vague whisper, some snippet of conversation. Maybe she'd noticed the cool reception after services the past couple of weeks.

I explained the sex questions, how she'd been there afterward, and how I couldn't shoo her away after I'd told her to see me, and how the others saw. And how we'd talked about her father's death, and yes, sex too.

"What are they saying you did?" Helen asked. She rubbed her hands over her face, then dropped them into her lap with a sigh. She seemed deflated—washed out, grim in her faded housedress. I should have hugged her, or simply touched her face, or her bare arms.

"Well, that's the tough part. They don't have any proof that *anything* happened. They just *think* something did . . . You know, I would never touch anyone besides you. God knows." I swallowed. "Touch her in that way."

"Yes, of course, yes," she said, hurrying toward the door to call the boys in. Then she suddenly stopped and turned toward me. "Did you want to? I know you didn't do anything, but did you want to?"

I sat with my head in my hands, not looking up. In the silence, she let the question go, and it never came up again.

She went to the door and called the boys.

"What happens now?" she asked. She turned and called the boys again, her voice breaking.

"Nothing, if they found my answers satisfactory." I knew they hadn't.

The boys finally came in, tumbling past us into the living room. I wrestled with them till we were all sweaty and panting. I pinned them both. Al grabbed his wrist and cried, ran off to his mother.

Helen and I were in a holding pattern in our sex life, which was not that unusual, based on what people had confided to me over the years. Having the kids, of course, changed things. Not like we'd had sex every night before prayers or anything, but the frequency had definitely dropped off.

To be honest, our marriage had hit a dead spot. As I lay in bed after prayer, I sometimes thought of other women. That night, and many others, I thought of Liz. Even later, when things got bad, I would think of me and Liz together, and it would provide a kind of solace. Maybe it was the devil's solace, but it was solace nevertheless.

"Now you've got them all riled up, and they'll never sleep," Helen said.

I knew she wouldn't sleep either, that neither of us would.

■ ■ ■

—What kind of tan do you get in hell?
—A Sa-tan.

After graduation from the seminary, I was assigned there, to the First Presbyterian Church of Detroit. In my second year, I met Helen, and in another year, we were married. On our wedding day, I was fulfilled spiritually, emotionally, physically—in every way.

The congregation seemed united back then. For a few years, I was their young, energetic minister, and Helen was my darling wife, active in the community, compassionate and idealistic. The women seemed to glow when we greeted them after services. The men shook my hand furiously, as if I had super strength they could pump out of me. And some days, I felt I had that strength. Everything seemed in sync. I was bringing people back, the congregation was expanding, diversifying. Helen and I had a sense of mission as we won them over. God seemed to be giving me extra wisdom. Baseball players talk about being in "the zone" where they can see pitches so clearly it seems like slow motion. I felt like I was in the ministers' "zone" then.

Helen had lived pretty far away, up in Rochester, which was mostly farmland then, so we were able to fall in love without much scrutiny. She was an old friend of my cousin's, and we met at a barbecue at her house. She shared my vision of a better, more peaceful world. Looking at her as objectively as I can, she was and continues to be a little naïve. That might not seem possible in light of what happened, but while I admit my idealism has faded and my spirit has been diminished, she is still steady and full of her belief in the goodness of mankind. She has a good heart—there's enough room in it for me, even now, though her stoic perseverance probably worked against me in the end. Everyone felt sorry for her. They thought her love for me had blinded her to the truth. How could they presume to know the truth?

In religious affairs, the truth does not always matter. If it's a matter of faith, then it's what you believe, regardless of proof. I was a little naïve too, thinking they had to have proof.

At dinner the next day, we held hands, as we always did before eating, and I prayed: "Father, bless this food and all those who sit at this table . . ." I continued my litany of the usual blessings and concerns, then finished up with, "Give us the strength to see this through. Let us pray that truth and goodness help keep us all safe, and that the innocent are . . . judged to be so. Amen."

A week later, the church council held a meeting to which I was not invited, and announced a second meeting, to which I was. I thought it best not to contact Liz. She'd stopped coming to class. I tried to ignore her absence, and we all glumly went through the motions. I stopped telling jokes.

Then, Liz ran away from home. They assumed that meant something *had* happened. What it meant was that the poor girl was getting hounded to death. If I'd thought about her instead of my position, maybe I would have contacted her and her family, explained to them what was happening—that some people wanted an excuse to give me trouble. Liz never admitted anything. She might have allowed that we got along well, and they seemed to have twisted that into something altogether less innocent. Neither of us ever mentioned that lone embrace, the embrace that aroused and tormented me.

Her mother called me when she ran away. "Have you heard from my daughter?" she asked.

"No, no I haven't."

"Listen, I know all that talk about her and you is a bunch of crap—excuse me, Reverend—but the poor girl's very upset. I'm worried sick."

I wanted to thank her. I admit, that was my first thought—that she believed in me. "If I hear anything, I'll call you immediately."

Helen was standing behind me. I turned to her. "That girl, Elizabeth, has run away."

Helen's frowned. "The poor girl," she said. "This will certainly be a test of everyone's faith . . . Do you think she'll try to call you?" Everything was a test of faith with her.

"No. No . . . I don't know." That night, Helen stayed up, I don't know how long. The next day, the dark circles around her eyes haunted me as I paced the kitchen. Maybe she stayed up to protect me, to protect our family, to protect me from myself. I was suffocating. I wanted to drive the streets, searching for Liz.

I should not be hard on Helen, for she has been my rock. The church is supposed to be the rock, but how, when my own church was turning me out, could I have found solace there?

■　■　■

—How many ministers does it take to screw in a lightbulb?

—Two. One to screw it in, and one to take up a collection for the burned-out bulb.

Liz returned after spending a night away, somewhere. She made no attempt to contact me. Helen got a baby-sitter, and she came with me to the meeting with the church council.

The only thing that ever surprised me about Helen was that she had smoked when she was younger. She told me this once with a thin smile, as if partially pleased at her one tiny rebellion. On the way to the meeting, I noticed the car ashtray slightly ajar, and the faint stale smell of smoke.

The meeting was more of the same, with Milton and Craig leading the way, labeling me "unresponsive" at the earlier encounter at my house. I wanted to punch Milton in the mouth. I knew things—his son was a drug dealer at the high school, for one. Turn the other cheek, I tried to tell myself, but my anger raged. I felt like I was back in the projects and somebody wasn't fighting fair—a kick in the balls. I may as well go down flaming, I thought, but Helen caught my eye and held it.

"I won't reply to any more of this slander," I said after two long hours of accusations and innuendo. I turned, took Helen's hand, and we left the room.

Most of us have lust in our hearts. We have to turn it around and channel it back into love for our chosen spouses. Catholic priests have it harder—they have to channel it back from the physical to a spiritual love. I always believed that being able to have sex, to have a wife, allowed me to be a better minister, to better understand the problems of my congregation. To avoid the attraction of the forbidden. But there's always something else forbidden that we want. Ask Adam and Eve.

God, my congregation, a beautiful wife, two sweet kids—you'd think that'd be enough to make anyone content. But I wanted more. Or maybe it was simply the chance to be a little reckless. Like Helen's cigarettes. Or maybe it'd just been a long day, and I had wanted comfort. Liz exuded sexuality, the hard bud of her body blossoming. Looking back, I'm sure I'd sent her signals in class. Inside, I knew I was guilty. God knew I was guilty. Given another chance, what would I have done with her?

■ ■ ■

—What's black and white and red all over?
—A minister caught with his pants down.

The final meeting, where they voted on whether I was to continue as their minister, was held immediately after a Sunday service that I hurried through. No one seemed to mind—they were there to vote, not to pray. I tried to show no fear as I led the congregation through the prayers and hymns, though I heard a quaver in my voice. I skipped the homily. I didn't want to try and manipulate God to save my ass. I would speak in my own defense later.

Anyone who wanted could rise and speak for or against me, with the "againsts" going first:

"As treasurer of the church council, I noticed a withdrawal from the general operating account. When I asked Reverend Stewart about this, he replied that he may have accidentally withdrawn money from the wrong account."

"My son said Reverend Stewart turned Bible school into a laughingstock, always cracking jokes about the holy book."

"We'll never know what happened between him and that girl, but can we even consider letting him stay on when we have these doubts?"

While listening to the "agins," I noticed the "fers" were lined up in equal numbers—I saw Elizabeth's mother in the line, but no sign of Liz herself. No one had mentioned the issue of race, but it was hanging in the air. I could feel it on my own skin as I counted the blacks and whites in each line.

A couple people had spoken on my behalf when Liz's mother stood.

"Reverend Stewart's been a . . . a good . . . good influence on my daughter growing up without a father. She told me . . . nothing happened between them, and I believe . . . ."

She wilted and collapsed to the hard floor. I heard her head thud against the tile. Helen had been standing at the end of the line. She quickly took charge. Some were saying Mrs. Taylor had just fainted, but Helen ordered them to call the paramedics. I was stunned and could only sit in front of the church and watch. People started to file out as the paramedics arrived, but Craig stood and shouted, "The meeting must continue, the meeting must continue!"

Those leaving turned. Some shook their heads and kept on going. I'd like to think those were my supporters leaving, those who had some dignity. A couple of people did continue to defend me while the paramedics worked on Mrs. Taylor, but their hearts weren't in it, I could tell. Helen was busy helping, so she never spoke. When I was asked to speak my piece, I hesitated, thinking about what I had put Liz and her mother through, what I'd put Helen through, about whether I could continue serving that congregation, whether I could serve God there any longer. It wasn't *our* kind of church—it was the same old church after all. By then, they had rushed Mrs. Taylor out of there, but still, I could not speak. "I have nothing to say," I said, though I have saved my prepared notes—I cannot let them go.

Mrs. Taylor had passed out and suffered a concussion when she fell. A small pool of blood lay where her head hit the tile. Helen rode in the ambulance with her.

I was asked to leave, and so I did. I drove home in silence, alone with the smell of Helen's cigarettes. I thought of Liz and broke down and wept. Poor Liz. My own problems seemed minor.

Later that evening, when the call came, I let Helen take it. "Don't give me any numbers," I said. "Yes or no?"

She shook her head. "I'm sorry, Jimmy." I sat there staring at the television—*Sixty Minutes*. Just their kind of story, I thought bitterly. I tried to focus on Liz's mother, her condition, but I kept coming back to me. What would *I* do now? Even then, I couldn't think proper thoughts.